Bigfoot, Dragons, Jesus Christ, and The Evolution of The Human Soul

CARLOS ABASCAL

Edition: First

ISBN: 979-8-89397-590-1

Published by Elite Scribes Book Writing

TABLE OF CONTENTS

PREFACE

This is a recount of my personal life experiences. As I lay in a dorm room bed at a youth hostel in Rome after having an energy-shifting dream that involved some personal inner struggles, during a solar flare on February 1 2025, I feel it is time to begin writing a book that many people told me I should write about my experiences.

I don't know where this is going to start and where it's going to end but that's about the story of my life so here we go.

PROLOGUE

This book is intended for people who already have some sort of spiritual or esoteric path or feel drawn to the subject of spirituality on the side of Light and Love in one way or another.

I am sharing my experiences as they have come to me with the intention that the stories here will reach the correct audience who will benefit from this book, and my hope is that it will reach those who are ready and able to interpret and receive its content.

There are many resources regarding the meaning and existence of Sasquatch beings, the esoteric significance of Dragons, and the interpretation of religion.

This book is not intended to prove or disprove the existence of anything. I am only sharing my experiences as I have lived them, and I'm focusing on the messages and understanding I have personally received. The scientific study of those subjects is a much broader and ongoing process of discovery and interpretation that will not be covered in this book. Terms to understand:

- Grid Work = Blessing The Land

- Light Portals = Spiritual Openings Of The Divine Essence

- Dark Portals = Spiritual Openings Of Negative Energy

- Opening Portals = Establishing An Energetic Or Spiritual Flow In A Specific Location

- Activation = Empowering Someone Spiritually and Through Cognitive Understanding to Step Into A New Role.

- Hearing From The Sasquatch = Receiving Telepathic Communication From The Sasquatch

- Light Language = Non-Cognitive Verbal Prayers Based On Spiritual Connection Similar To Biblical "Tongues"

- Channeling = To Receive and Deliver Messages Coming From the Spiritual Realm

- Downloads = Hidden Knowledge, Or Divine Wisdom Or Direction

CHAPTER ONE
My First Sasquatch Story

I go into the woods to hike to remote spots and camp. I love waterfalls, hot springs and nice views. This time, I was in a Canyon by myself in Oregon, camping. I drove from Idaho and was in unfamiliar territory after exploring a waterfall during the day.

I had seen a trail halfway on the way down to the waterfall trailhead, and I knew there was a campsite there. When I came back up from the waterfall, I was the last person to get out of the area, and it was almost sunset. By the time I found the campsite, it was starting to get dark and cold. I have this thing for hiking at night without lights.

One time, I hiked 9 miles one way to Kraemer Lake near Redfish Lake in Idaho at night without lights. I do that a lot, especially during a full moon.

I enjoy the peace and silence, and I often get into a meditative state while doing it. I like to play the Native American flute or a portable didgeridoo while I hike as well, which adds a lot to my hikes at night. Sometimes I do freak a lot of campers out as I hike past their tents without lights. It's almost funny to feel like a Bigfoot in the dark without being one, so I can relate a little bit.

Now, back to my Oregon encounter. The Forest was super dark, there was no moon, and I was cooking dinner with my gas stove. Normally, I camp without a campfire to prevent forest fires.

When I was done eating, I decided to start playing my Didgeridoo. If you don't know what a didgeridoo is, it's an Australian Aboriginal wind instrument. It is played using circular breathing and projecting animal noises and rhythms, toots, and other sounds.

The sound is deep and long, and it's considered a spiritual instrument. I played for a while, maybe 30 minutes, and was enjoying playing in the dark without lights and looking at the stars. I was feeling really good and then decided to get my speaker and play some electronic music. This is when things got weird.

As soon as I turned the speaker on, I heard a horrendous scream from about 75 feet into the woods. It was super loud, and it was most definitely not an animal sound I had ever heard.

It sounded like King Kong hit his toe on the side of a tree; it resounded and echoed through the mountains, and the whole forest was absolutely quiet.

I felt that whatever made that noise wanted me to turn the electronic music off. I grabbed my stuff, threw it in the car, and tried to leave.

I started my car and tried to put my phone in its holder. The presence of whatever it was felt very real and very heavy, and I locked myself in the car.

I was going to Google my way out, but the phone holder broke, and I realized I had no reception without it. I was not going to find the right trail to get out of there, since the road was so rocky, and I was so deep in the canyon, so I decided to stay the night.

I turned my car off and I waited for a while, listened from my car and rolled down the window a little, and looked into the dark woods, but there was no movement.

All I could see were the stars in the sky at the top of the trees. I sat in my car until I got bored and strapped my hunting knife on my belt and walked out of the car without lights.

By now, it was cold, and there was absolutely no noise of any kind. I leaned against my car and waited in the dark with my hand on my knife. I didn't want to take any guns across state lines from Idaho, so that's all I had.

I had heard of people taking down bears with a knife, and I have a fairly large two-sided Spanish dagger-type hunting knife; it is very pointy, and I was ready to pull it out and start stabbing if I sensed anything coming at me. I'm an instructor on traditional Spanish sword fighting, and I know how to use a knife; besides, I don't know that I could actually point and shoot down anything in such a dark forest.

My instinct told me to walk in the dark 3 times around the perimeter of my campsite, so I did so to set my boundary. I did it and sat up against my car afterward, listening intently for any noise.

I don't ever remember hearing such silence except for when I've camped in the desert. After what seemed like an eternity, I relaxed a little, and I then walked for a good 200 feet down the trail that I took to drive up to the campsite. I stood there and waited.

I knew something or someone was closely watching me; I could feel it, but I couldn't see any movement. By this time, I was relaxed but stayed aware.

When I play in the forest, at night, the sound carries very far and echoes in the distance, and maybe whatever screamed at me heard my didgeridoo and came to check out what it was.

I realized that my Didgeridoo playing did not bother whatever screamed at me, but the electronic music did. I stood in the dark, far from my car, waiting and listening, and pondering on what could possibly happen next.

Most people I've heard reports of try to run and get away, but I couldn't leave on foot or drive away, so there I was, alone, quiet, and walking without lights near whatever this thing was.

Since they say that Sasquatch is telepathic, maybe it knew I was not a threat as long as I wasn't attacked, or maybe it thought I was completely crazy and didn't want to have anything to do with me. In my mind, I thought over and over how to stab it quickly in certain artery spots. I'm only 5'7" and 185 lbs of pure lean muscle and quite sexy for sure. Maybe it was a hairy female Sasquatch looking for some love.

Anyways, back to my story, I normally use a camping hammock and I have camped all over the Pacific Northwest including all of British Columbia on the way back to Idaho from Oregon and Washington on the Canadian side, and even slept through some crazy Canadian hail storms since my hammock set up has an excellent rain fly attachment. But I was not going to willingly turn myself into a hammock burrito for that thing to eat! Not tonight, "lady Sasquatch!!" So I slept in my car.

The night took forever to be over, and I barely slept at all. I felt like this thing was looking at me all night while I tried to sleep. I figured, if it attacked me, it was going to have to deal with the shell of my car first.

I got out of there early in the morning. Then, when I got home, I looked up Sasquatch sounds on YouTube, and I found one that sent chills down my spine. It was EXACTLY WHAT I HEARD! It wasn't a bear, it wasn't a cat, it sounded like a seal and a monkey at the same time, and the thing had to be at least 700 to 900 lbs.

I started researching everything about Sasquatch since then, and I know now I have had two more encounters, which at the time I didn't know I was having. I even have pictures I took of a Sasquatch structure in Idaho and of some huge footprints as well.

CHAPTER TWO
My Second Sasquatch Story

This story happened around the year 2000, also in Oregon. It seems like every time I go to Oregon, I have a weird encounter of some sort.

I have had a conversation with a shape-shifting alien there, and swatted a fairy as I was sitting next to a friend who saw it come up and fly right in front of my face at a didgeridoo festival near the coast.

I also saw a huge UFO right above my head as I was sleeping in my hammock near Corvallis one night, and the list goes on and on. I think Oregon is a really mystical place, but I don't know what sort.

I have lots of weird stories to tell, but I'll stick to the Sasquatch story for now.

At the time, I was living in a different state, and I had met a lady online in a chat room way before the internet was much of a thing, and dating apps did not exist back then.

Honestly, I don't even know how we started talking, nor how we found each other again, but we did. Talk about a blind date, there were no profile pictures back then, so I really didn't know what I was getting into. The lady I met later became my first wife, and this was our first trip together.

We drove towards the Oregon coast after my arrival at the Redmond airport, and by the time we found a hotel, it was late and dark.

This would have been in the early fall, so there wasn't much rain at the time.

The hotel was somewhere near the coast. I remember there was a restaurant bar across the street, and the hotel was creepy. It was painted light blue on the outside, and the paint was peeling off. The room we stayed in was painted orange all throughout, and the bed covers and sheets were orange too.

We decided to go for a night ride after checking in at the hotel to get to know each other, and the forest on both sides of the road was quite thick and dark.

We drove and drove and talked and talked for a long time, and we were listening to 'The Doors' album and the song called Riders on the Storm.

Everything seemed surreal in Oregon for some reason. The feeling was similar to being in "The Twilight Zone" show from way back when.

At some point, we decided to try to find a place to stop, rest, and start heading back to the hotel, and we found a parking lot on the right side of the road near a lake, where we pulled over.

I had a weird feeling when we first pulled up, and I was hesitant to get out of the car, but she kept insisting. It was really dark, and there were stars, but the moon wasn't shedding much light, and I was a bit uneasy, but I couldn't pinpoint why I was feeling that way.

We finally got out of the car and were sitting on the hood, talking for maybe a minute or two, when all of a sudden we heard something crashing through the brush, coming up a steep, wooded path from the lake. It was almost a sheer drop to the lake, definitely not a grade someone could easily walk up without risking a fall.

This was no small animal, and as I remember trying to describe it back then, I remember saying that it sounded like King Kong was making his way through the forest.

We both heard it since it was so loud. There were tree branches being broken and tons of commotion as this thing made its way through the dark forest toward the road that was behind us.

The road was a two-lane highway, and on the other side, there was a tall wall. I would say the wall was almost 90 degrees steep and maybe about 40 feet high, and there were really tall trees on top, and its face was completely flat.

My girlfriend and I started freaking out, she started screaming when I all of a sudden decided to walk towards it to check what it was. I had no lights nor weapons, and I was heading into the dark towards whatever it was we were hearing as this massive thing made its way.

She then screamed, "It may be a deer!!" and this, for some reason, made me stop and run back to the car.

I got inside and started the engine and forgot that the car had an issue with her side of the door so she couldn't get inside and started freaking out. I put the car in park and got out to go to her side of the car to open her door for her as she ran to the driver's side to try to get away and put the car between her and the noise at the end of the parking lot. We were definitely doing a life-and-death midnight Chinese fire drill while we were trying to get in the car.

There was silence for a couple of seconds as we finally opened her door, and we stood there for a second listening before getting in the car, and heard nothing for what could have been a couple of seconds, but seemed like an eternity.

We finally got in the car, rolled the windows down, and tried to point at whatever it was with our headlights, and all of a sudden, we heard the same sounds of thrashing through the brush that we had heard before except, it was no way up on the trees and this really freaked us out so I stepped on the gas and we took off heading back towards the creepy hotel where we came from. That's when things got even weirder.

As we were driving along the road while trying to stay calm, we started talking about what it could have been.

We noticed that there was a very unusual fog on the road, the stereo was playing the same song, "Riders on the Storm," and the fog was not the kind of fog that hits your windshield so that you can't see in front of you.

It was more like a tunnel opening up right in front of us, but made of fog.

I don't remember ever seeing fog like this before. It was really odd. As we were driving, we were trying to figure out what could have made such noise, and nothing made any sense.

First, she mentioned that deer or elk do not break brush like that and plow through everything in their path.

We also didn't hear any hooves cross the road, and there was no way anything could have climbed the wall on the other side of the road so fast without causing a rock slide.

We also didn't see any shadows, as there were cars going by when we were exiting the parking lot. It was almost as if whatever it was, leaped from our side of the road to the top of the wall and started climbing onto the trees, and we figured it was too tall of a wall for any bear to jump that high, and this was no small animal at all.

As we were having these realizations, the music kept playing and she almost started going into a panic and mentioned that she wished we were back at the hotel and all of a sudden, as in a blink of an eye, there was the same bar on the right of the road and the creepy hotel on the left.

But how could this be possible that quickly? We literally had just left the parking lot, and we were already back at the hotel in no time. Maybe 20 minutes at best. Nothing made sense.

We went inside, and the eerie feeling was completely unshakeable, so we sat there in the orange living room, trying to make sense of what had just happened and coming to no reasonable conclusions.

At this time, I had never heard of Bigfoot, and I had no idea of any of the stuff that had just happened, so I told her to stay at the hotel and told her I was thinking I should drive back to the place to see if I could figure it out.

She became scared and absolutely did not want to let me drive back out there alone, so she suggested we should spend the night, calm ourselves down, have breakfast the next day, and then head over and try to find the same place in the morning.

That was the most sensible thing I had heard that night. We felt weird all together through the night but managed to get some sleep, and in the morning, after having breakfast, we started heading back over to try to find the parking lot by the lake.

We remembered that we had made no turns at all on the way there the night before, and it should have been easy to find this lake and the parking lot next to it, so we started driving.

We drove and paid close attention to everything the whole way, and we passed many places and towns. We at least drove for well over an hour in one direction without making any turns, and we could not believe we weren't able to find it so far. Finally, after an hour and a half drive, we came up to the place.

There was a lot of debris and broken branches right where we heard the noise, but we didn't see anything unusual, although it was the same parking lot for sure.

What made the whole thing even more strange was that it took us no time to drive back to the hotel from the same spot the night before, as we were traveling inside this weird tunnel of fog, but it took an hour and a half to find the place the next day, coming from the opposite direction.

Now that I have had other encounters and I have listened to so many stories on different channels and other sources, I realize that the only thing that could make sense would be a Sasquatch coming up from the lake beside us.

In that case, everything would make sense. What blows me away to think about is that the leap it took from one side of the road to the top of the trees across the road and uphill was something that no animal could do.

Welcome to the "Twilight Zone."

CHAPTER THREE
The Water Witch

It had been a long time since I wrote my first two stories a couple of years ago, and what has transpired since then keeps evolving in many weird ways.

Sometime after I wrote the last story, I met another lady online. She sent me a friend request because we had some friends in common from the energy healing and metaphysical communities I was involved with.

My spiritual path took some shape in a Christian realm, but as I developed spiritual gifts, I kept getting kicked out of churches, and that's how I ended up in the metaphysical communities.

Anyhow, I've seen a lot of weird things all my life, and nothing really surprises me anymore.

The lady eventually became a friend, and we started traveling together. She does water blessings, grid work opening portals of positive energy through the land, and activates people in light language or what is considered tongues in the Christian realm.

We both have very special capabilities and I took the leap of faith to travel with her and it was a really crazy train for me to travel with her as she drives like a speed demon while holding her cell phone in her hand because she's half blind and reads the written step directions on google maps instead of having a holder and using navigation.

Yes, this brought a whole other meaning to WTH altogether as I had to sit with my eyes closed for hours at a time till we got to wherever we were going. I've never seen anyone drive 80, weaving in and out of lanes during rush hour traffic in Salt Lake City while casually chatting and nearly missing a ton of cars as she flew by.

This was not for the faint of heart, and she's been doing it for decades, traveling through the whole country and has a ton of tickets everywhere, and I have the underwear to prove it. If I had a penny for every time I said the F word, I'd buy myself a plane ticket back home in first class. I don't even know where she gets the energy to do all she does, and her chatter… well, it just won't stop.

We traveled several times to Arizona, once to a Native American wedding where the main chief leading the ceremony, thought he was in Arkansas and didn't know how he ended up in Arizona to preside over the wedding in a giant teepee and he didn't even know there was a wedding and the bride and groom didn't know him.

Somehow, the wedding assembled last minute, and it was absolutely out of this world. The wedding took place at a private hot springs in a native American reservation in the Arizona desert, where you could see Mexico from there, and there were a lot of hot pools to choose from. It was really a magical place.

They brought the giant teepee out of nowhere, set it up, and provided yummy food for everyone. There were many native Americans there hosting storytelling circles, and many other activities, and the Hotsprings were just amazing.

As we sat in a circle inside the teepee, there was a staff with feathers, and it had the head of a falcon at the top. There was a lot of native chanting, and later there was a huge peyote and drumming ceremony where they kept serving peyote tea over and over all night long, and things got really crazy.

I was really high from the peyote tea most of the night, and sporadically, I would get the urge to get up and start playing the didgeridoo as the drumming continued non-stop, and many supernatural things were happening, and it went on till sunrise. Everyone came out of that teepee like they had been fumigated with DDT.

After several trips to Utah, Hawaii, Arizona, and tons of crazy events that would take a lifetime to write, we ended up at a metaphysical Sasquatch gathering of sorts in Northern Washington.

Now, I had had enough of driving with my lady friend, and I needed some peace and quiet, so I drove my car alone.

I was the first person to get to the campsite, and since there was no one there yet, I decided to go find a place to camp in the forest.

As I was going up a dirt road, I got a strong feeling that I should take a trail to my left. Eventually, I reached a small bridge over a creek, and there was a perfect spot where I could set up my rooftop tent and spend the night.

I set up my table and chair under my awning to have lunch, and I noticed directly in front of me, an opening into the forest, and for some reason, I knew there was going to be Sasquatch activity there. I could feel it, but I still can't explain it. It's like a knowing of sorts. As I explored, I found a stump with a large quartz stone sitting on top as a table offering of sorts.

At least that's what it felt like to me. As I looked around, I noticed all sorts of anomalies with the trees around. It seemed like someone had placed them to form barriers, arches, and pyramids with trees upside down.

As I went further to investigate, I found several Sasquatch footprints. This was definitely not a regular healthy forest where all the trees point up and look all the same. And the vibe there was quite intense, to say the least.

I eventually went back to my spot, spent the rest of the night, and headed the next morning to the event. I really wanted to mingle with other folk, but I wanted quiet sleep, so I camped at a more secluded spot away from where my friend could find me, but she still found me!! I tried to ignore her because if I didn't, I wasn't going to get rid of her.

I started meeting and introducing myself to the new people who had arrived for the event. As the event unfolded over the following few days, I realized that these people had encounters with the Sasquatch that were far beyond what most people experienced.

Most people I had heard of were the hiking and hunting types who run into Sasquatch for the first time, go into a panic and run, and don't say anything for a long time to anyone for fear of being ridiculed, or similar stories.

These folk at the event were sharing experiences they had with the Sasquatch that were more long-term, personal, and metaphysical and some even had written books about the Sasquatch from a spiritual perspective and many of them mentioned that there is a connection between the Sasquatch, supernatural phenomena, other beings like the dogman and skinwalker ranch events, or even fairies and alien phenomena. It was eye-opening for me.

As the event unfolded, I met several people including a Native American lady who during the event was gifted three strands of Sasquatch hair, one white, one black, and one brown that were left at her chair during the event, she told me the Sasquatch gifted them to her and no one knew about it.

Also, she mentioned to me that the Sasquatch can cloak themselves, and they can be standing next to you and you wouldn't even know, which was amazing for me to hear, but it was more amazing to hear that the Sasquatch had told her that humans can do it too.

We saw orbs at night while hiking without lights under the moonlight, heard noises all around the camp, some people saw the Sasquatch and fairies, and we all shared our stories and drummed and played music around the fire. The activities at the event were lovely.

There were several presentations for different modalities of healing, and I even felt like I was supposed to do a presentation of sorts so I got put on the schedule and I had to wait till the last minute for my spirit guide Jesus himself to tell me what to do except he didn't, so I ended up sharing some of my stories and doing a spiritual activation that was quite powerful. Ok, maybe he did tell me, but it came in the form of a hunch in my heart.

It was almost unreal to hear how so many of these folk had long-term relations with the forest people and how their connection with them had given them spiritual understanding.

Toward the end of the 4-day event, I went back to the same mountain where I had found the structures, but this time I drove to the ridge and found a giant 100ft plus symmetrical structure and took many photos and videos examining how it was built.

I recorded footprints, and I knew I was onto something more than just a random encounter. It seemed like I was being shown these structures for a reason.

I recalled finding another huge structure in Idaho a couple of years before, on the other side of a remote lake, only reachable by boat while camping with a different lady friend.

The way that these structures were built defied human capabilities as it would have required machinery to lift the massive trees to build them and to perfectly balance a massive tree at the top of the structures.

It would also have required road access to get where I found them, and those places were quite remote with no trails or vehicle access nearby. This was the beginning of my journey, which keeps taking new facets as I go further. I felt I was slowly being ushered into a mysterious new world.

CHAPTER FOUR
My Childhood Dragon

Way back when I was a 7-year-old kid, and I'm not going to mention the year because I'll date myself, I was invited to go to a town in a faraway village where my school friend's mom grew up.

I was a pretty adventurous kid and by this age, I had already paid for a trip for my mom and I to Acapulco for a week with hotel, transportation, food, and many smoothies by teaming up with her as she made sandwiches for me to go sell at the office buildings in our city.

I made so much money during the school vacation months selling sandwiches that my basket was always full of cash. By now she was used to letting me loose and do unusual things that most kids my age never dream of doing.

Back to my story at the mountains, as my friend and I arrived at the village after a grueling chicken bus trip, I was immediately enchanted with the mountains and the open spaces since I had been raised in an urban area.

I had tons of cash on me for a 7-year-old and decided I wanted to rent a donkey so I wouldn't have to walk to the village up in the mountains where my friend's mom lived. Now that I think about it, what 7-year-old kid does that?

As we were halfway up the mountain, I was making fun of my friend who had to walk, and the donkey got spooked by something and ran all the way back to where I had rented it, with me hanging on to it for dear life, so I actually had to do the trip again on foot. I was so mad, and my friend kept laughing at me, which made me even more mad.

As we finally reached the village, the views were something to behold.

I'd never hiked long distances, let alone seen the beauty of the mountains, and I for sure had never rented a donkey.

The village was very small, with just a few rustic houses and lots of space for us kids to play and explore. It was definitely a first experience for me. The following day, my friend and I were out playing, and I had picked up a machete that they used to cut firewood with.

I remember he had mentioned he had a catholic charm around his neck for protection. I had no grid for any religion, so it didn't register with me until something really strange happened. I remember he had picked up a rock and almost got stung by a scorpion.

I don't remember if I tried to swing the machete at the scorpion or if later I was just swinging it but I remember it left my hands as I swung it and it went spinning through the air directly at my friend and just before it cut his head off, it stopped in mid-air as if it was stopped by an invisible force and it fell straight down to the ground. It was really odd.

Now that I look back, I can tell there was a lot of paranormal activity on those mountains, beginning with the incident with the donkey.

People ask me all the time how I remember all that and all I can say is that I was one of those kids that was fully aware really early in life, so much so that I still have fresh memories of when I was 6 months old and by the time I was 1 year old, I knew 13 songs as well as my full name, address and phone number and I could perfectly speak and walk and pick wallets out of people's pockets. Maybe because there weren't so many vaccines at the time. Ok, I didn't pickpocket, that was a joke.

Back to my story at the mountains.

Towards the next day's evening, after we arrived, the sun started to set, and we noticed a group of about six or seven kids who were staring down at something in the valley. They were pointing while one of them kept swinging a machete in the air, and whatever they were looking at kept them very attentive.

As my friend and I approached, we all could see a giant cloud as wide as a freeway and what could have been at least a couple of miles long at the bottom of the mountains moving like a snake at the edge of the ground between two buttes. Mind that we were a group of about 8 to 10 kids looking at the same thing, ages ranging from 4 years old to about 10.

I asked what that thing was that we were looking at, and they explained to me that this was a dragon spirit that took the form of a cloud that would come to the area every so often, and it would destroy the crops.

They had a legend that when this started to happen, the priest of the town sent a boy and a girl to the top of the mountain. The boy with a machete and the girl with scissors cut the sign of the cross in the air towards the dragon cloud, and it would go away.

I listened in amazement and disbelief, but at the same time, I was looking at this giant cloud slither between the faraway buttes in the valley and heading toward us, and we all saw it.

I don't know what got into me but I asked if I could swing the machete and as soon as I started swinging, there was a thud in the air between us and the dragon in the distance, similar to the energetic thuds in the movie The Matrix and as soon as this happened, the dragon cloud turned around and left where it came from, right in front of all of us.

Don't ask me how that is even possible because I can't explain it either. All I know is something we all saw, and this puzzled me for many years to come.

CHAPTER FIVE
The Dragons Come Back

Many years later, after my childhood experience with the dragon, I happened to embark on a spiritual mission trip to the Big Island of Hawaii. Another magical place with a volcano spirit called Pelé, with my crazy friend, I had been traveling (the one who drives like a maniac). I actually appreciate her friendship a lot, but I still like to give her a hard time.

The island is very different from the other Hawaiian Islands I've been to, since it is surrounded mostly by high rocky cliffs. This is a place where lots of personal shadow work takes place. The energy on the island brings out your shadow side to be exposed and healed. Anyone who knows about this place can confirm that the energy there is something extraordinary.

As soon as we arrived and got settled in the evening, we headed to greet and bless the spirit of the volcano. I had brought my Native American flute to play and do ceremony, and the views of the lava were breathtaking. We had been traveling on and off for quite some time, and our shadow sides were definitely starting to show.

She insisted that I not eat hamburgers because they brought out a nasty side in me, and during the trip. She also had a crazy meltdown with the energies of the island, so I had to go alone for a walk and get some space to relax. Traveling together was always very intense and not always as easy or pleasant as we both have strong spiritual energies and wills.

During my solo walk along the rocky cliffs of the island, I stumbled upon an older lady who was sitting on a chair on the rocky surface facing the ocean. She was a lifetime local, and as I was walking by, she turned and looked at me with a knowing smile as if she had been waiting for me the whole time, and she asked me to do her a favor.

It was odd to sense that this was not your regular old lady or situation, but I agreed and asked what she needed. Now that I think about it, she may have been the incarnated spirit of Pelé.

She asked me if I would accompany her in smoking a joint that she had, which I was not expecting at all from an old lady, but I needed to relax, so I accepted the invitation, and we started talking while looking at the ocean. She then offered me to drink some hard liquor, but I declined because I don't drink, and she was amazed that I didn't drink.

She said something along the lines of "You are a very unique individual," and I was thinking to myself, "Why, because I'm not a drunk?" She let me have the rest of the joint, which I thanked her for as I walked away. I put the joint away since I'm more of a "One-hit wonder," or in other words, not a professional pot smoker, but oh man, that stuff was good!

As I walked into the pine trees that you often find at the beaches on the Big Island, I noticed what seemed to be a memorial to a young man who had passed away recently. His photo was above the writing of his life on paper that was nailed to a tree, and flowers sat all over as a memorial to his life.

Suddenly, I don't know if the weed hit me or if the Spirit hit me or both, but I took out my Native American flute and started playing this amazing tune that I had never played.

People started gathering from all around the beach, standing in the distance listening, and all of a sudden, I felt the most absolute connection with the spirit of the island as it went through my whole being.

I then started singing in what seemed to me a beautiful tune in what sounded like the Hawaiian language, except I don't know how to speak Hawaiian, and it was not something I had ever heard, but it was, for lack of better words, the essence of the beautiful spirit of the island. This went on for about 20 minutes, and people were just standing around like this happens every day, and seemed to know the tune I was singing, even though I had never heard it in my life, and I could never remember it nor emulate it again if I tried. Man, that weed was good!! I thought to myself as I walked further towards the cliffs and went back to playing my flute. The vibe was absolutely majestic and unreal. Beautiful sunny skies, light breeze, and the sound of the crashing waves in the distance.

I noticed a cloud in the sky that was very different from all the other puffy clouds. The cloud was static and had the distinct shape of a dragon's face, and it was directly in front of what perfectly looked like a winged angel. I played my flute and enjoyed the experience for a good 30 minutes.

As I played, I noticed that these two cloud beings, the dragon and the angel, had not moved an inch, but all the other puffy clouds around had come and gone.

I took many pictures of these Dragon and Angel clouds that I still have on my phone, and I even set one as my home screen. The whole time I was there, the clouds didn't move or change shape, and I wondered what this all could mean.

At first, I thought it was a spiritual battle between good and evil as the dragon is always depicted in Christian mythology as an evil spirit but the more I fell into the energy of the clouds, the more I realized that there was no conflict and the realization came to me that they were dancing or playing together. When I realized this, I had a download of sorts that was very loud in my spirit and very real.

It showed me that this dragon was my childhood dragon and that it was my ally and protector, and I had been fighting it my whole life. Tears were rolling down my face as I remembered my childhood experience and how much it puzzled and haunted me throughout my life.

This showed me such love that it went through my bones, and I had no words, nor had I ever experienced what was happening. At that moment, I had a deeply transformative experience, and a peace came over me which was very settling and unshakable.

Many religious groups say the spirit of the big island is a demon but I was shown clearly that it is a regional angelic being of healing and transformation assigned to hold the healing energy frequency of the island for people to transform and grow spiritually and this event was just the beginning of what was yet to come.

CHAPTER SIX
Jesus Christ

My first spiritual experiences happened by themselves when I was a kid. My mom used to take me to the park in the afternoons, and I remember looking as the sun was about to set behind the trees, somehow realizing that there was a God.

I started praying on my own, but my family was never the religious type, so all my experiences were more organic, and they began with occurrences like the dragons and so on. At least I knew I was being protected and that I was connected, but I had no way to explain it in words. By the time I turned 18, I had moved out of the house, and my solo journey began.

I got a job working at a retail store as a cashier and another job working as a bank teller, and I bought myself a motorcycle before I knew how to ride it. Everyone thought that was crazy, and they were worried about my riding, and soon I found out why.

I had been riding like a speed demon without a helmet for a month and one day, I went into a speed wobble, flew off my bike, and hit the pavement with my face as I watched my bike slide all over the freeway, throwing sparks everywhere. I got up and walked over to my bike, and the highway patrol was already there.

I don't even know how they got there so quickly. They didn't let me get on the bike; they called an ambulance and told me that the speedometer had stopped at 85 miles per hour and that I was lucky to be alive.

They didn't write me a ticket and the paramedics could not find anything wrong with me, they kept poking my ribs looking for broken bones and it was tickling me to death and they found no broken bones and all I had was just the gash on my face from the pavement which only took a few stitches to fix and I was later released with bandages on my face. The doctors told me that I only needed 16 stitches, but they gave me 19 to remind me of this.

Shortly after that accident, I lost both jobs since I had no transportation, and I soon started dating a girl from work, and we moved in together and bought a car. Later, we broke up, and I kept the car. It was an old 1979 AMC Hornet with high miles, and it was a complete piece of junk.

Eventually, I got a job which I was hoping would be temporary, working for a convenience store chain, and got assigned to a store in a gang-infested black neighborhood working graveyard shift by myself. During the first week, I had many local people come to ask me if I had been robbed yet.

This gave me time to make friends with the many private armed security guards who came to get coffee at night. I told them they could take anything they wanted any time, which was a smart move, and I made friends with all of them, and they kept coming for free coffee and donuts, of course.

Then the first robbery happened, and I found myself with a Uzi (a small machine gun) pointing at my face. As time went by, I realized I was in a war zone, so I got an iron putter for kids and hid it behind the counter.

Every time anyone came to rob the store, I would whip it out, jump over the counter, and start swinging at the robbers, and over the next couple of years, I became a master at working with the cops to get people arrested for robbery. It was a miracle that I didn't get killed. I went through shootings, robberies, riots, and everything that happened in those lovely parts of town.

The security guards and the cops knew me really well, and they even invited me to their parties. It felt almost as if I was one of them, and I was proud to have put so many people in jail.

I would clock in at 10 at night and blast heavy metal music all night long to pump me up for the next robbery. I had collected a ton of surveillance videotapes from the robberies at the store and a ton of subpoenas for the court that got the robbers many years to regret robbing my friendly neighborhood store.

The word got around and the robbers finally started robbing other stores and left me alone because the security guards where the robbers lived, had the police scanner on all the time and were the first ones to respond when I called 911 after a robbery and all they had to do was wait till the robbers came back running to their house to be intercepted by the security guards with their batons in hand.

I became enraged and hateful, and I wanted to hit everybody with my iron putter.

The whole time, I was dropping off applications at Home Depot and other places, looking for work that didn't involve this environment.

I made friends with some born-again Christians who were always praying for my safety and inviting me to their homes. I thought their church pastor was a weirdo, and I attended several times, but I could not see myself being part of that crowd.

Two years went by, and I finally decided to apply for a job in a county far away from that nasty place, and by a miracle, I got a job doing data entry for a healthcare management company near the coast. What a change!

I lived by the beach now, and things were going well, except that I had tremendous PTSD from my time working at the store, and it was affecting my new job.

When I put in my resignation at the store, the old lady who managed it told me that I had come in such a good boy, and I had become a heart-hardened cop.

That was an understatement, and I realized I needed help. I never got into any drinking or drugs, but I had hell inside me. I instinctively knew that something had shifted in me and that God could bring me back to normal, but I didn't know where to start.

I was extremely oppressed, depressed, fearful, and angry all at the same time. I had lived through deadly circumstances for 2 years, and I decided to give churches a try, so I looked up a church and attended a Calvary Chapel youth meeting. All I remember is that I was sitting alone, at the back of the church and sobbing uncontrollably. I didn't feel welcome or seen.

Eventually, a young so-called "prayer warrior" came to ask me a few questions, and he asked me if I was able to forgive, and I told him no. He just walked away and said, "Dude, you have some hardcore problems, keep reading your bible and coming," and I never saw him again.

I got into surfing and moved a block away from the beach.

I lived in a party area, and everything was great except my insides. I kept running into this ad on TV about a Brazilian church that claimed lots of crazy things like miracles, freedom from demonic oppression, the release of witchcraft and Santeria, and many other things, so I decided to give it a try.

I needed help badly. The rage inside of me was unbearable.

I ended up attending a service, and all they did was pray for people really loudly.

I came in sobbing uncontrollably again, and this caught the attention of one of the pastors, who came and prayed for me really hard, shaking my head like they do in Tijuana when they shove a bottle of tequila down your throat while blowing a whistle in your ear.

My hair was a mess after the prayer, and I didn't feel much, but when I left, I noticed that I could suddenly see colors and smell the wind and the trees, and it was the first time in a long time that I was able to sleep. I kept going to that place and noticed many changes in me that were nothing short of supernatural.

As time went by, I felt much better and decided it was time to get rid of all the death metal and satanic music I was addicted to, so I brought all my cassettes in 3 large, hefty trash bags.

I got rid of hundreds of complete albums that day. All the collections of Slayer, Megadeath, Black Sabbath, Dio, Ozzy Osborne, Pantera, Decide, and others which are just my favorite music to be able to go to sleep. The underground heavy metal and death metal collection came next. I made friends with another kid who decided he wanted to join the church as a deacon, and he kept telling me that every time I left, I would miss out because someone got an exorcism.

I could not believe my ears, and I decided to stay one day, and lo and behold, they were praying for a lady who was manifesting some serious Santeria demons. I rushed to try to help, and the pastor told me not to touch her, but it was too late. As she got set free, I started feeling really weird, and I told the pastor what I was feeling, and he prayed for me.

As soon as he put his hand on my head and started shaking it like a maraca, I went down kicking and screaming, and I wanted to kill the pastor. I remember being held to the ground by several people and sounding like an enraged werewolf, and finally, something came out of me like a dirty sock from my feet to my head.

I lay there speechless, noticing an angry entity hovering above my body that felt so familiar that I thought for a moment that it was me, but I was on the other side, lying on the floor. I instinctively knew that it came from the music I used to listen to, and it left, and I finally went home, and all I could do was lie in bed for days.

Whatever happened at that church was so powerful that it wiped me out, but I eventually regained my strength and felt so much better, so I decided to become religious… and that's when things got weird.

CHAPTER SEVEN
The Beach Bums

As I began what I thought was my religious journey, I kept attending this Brazilian church, which later turned out to be a cult. I started telling everyone about Jesus, including my family. I did witness quite a few events that would be considered miraculous, and my grandma and my mom became believers, and so did other people in my family. I lived in the heavy-duty party zone of the coast, so I spent my days surfing, partying, and going to church, but I didn't care for drugs or alcohol. It was the perfect life for a while, but as I became more and more religious, I started donating all my stuff, including all my money, car, and credit cards.

All I knew was that I felt way better, and I was starting to enjoy life at the beach a lot.

The parties started daily from Tuesday to Saturday, and Sunday and Monday were for trash cleanup. I became a really good ping pong player and surfer, and I kept attending the church services and telling people about the stuff I saw at the church, and they all thought I was crazy.

I just couldn't imagine life without surf, parties, and church. I felt God all over me all the time, and I really didn't have a clue what to do with my life.

As time went on, I kept running into two surfer brothers who were beach bums, and they were Christians as well. They kept telling me to get out of that Brazilian church that I had been attending because it was a cult, except I had never seen so many miracles and crazy things happen at any other church except for that one.

One day, I was riding my beach cruiser to go surf up the street, and it had a surfboard rack on the back. As I was crossing the street on the crosswalk, a 16-year-old girl who had just gotten her driver's license came plowing through the left lane as I was crossing in the middle of the street and ran me over and I totaled her car on impact as I landed on her hood and roof.

My left lower leg broke in half. I had an open compound fracture, and the bones were sticking out. I woke up in the middle of the road with my face on the hot pavement, looking down the street and recognizing where I was, but at an angle that I had never seen. At this time, two people were next to me. One was putting his shirt over my leg, and the other was praying for me.

Later, I was told by some friends who saw the accident and gathered my stuff after the ambulance took me away that the only person that was there was the one putting his shirt on my leg, but I distinctively remember the other guy praying and as soon as he did, I felt power come through his hand and I woke up screaming because the pavement was red hot. I believe that guy had to have been an angel of sorts. I just don't understand why he didn't peel me off the pavement because I was cooking!!

I was taken to the hospital, where I asked the doctor if I would ever be able to surf again. As they were hauling me to surgery on a stretcher, he looked at my leg, and he said yes and said that he would do his best. That's all I cared about! Over the next month, I went through 10 reconstructive surgeries, a punctured lung, and they had to graft the abdominal muscles on my leg to make it shut.

Later, they had to re-open my abdomen to extract a blood clot the size of a softball. I started having nightmares from all the morphine that I was consuming, as the doctors just gave me a hose with a button that would dispense more morphine in case I felt pain, so I just taped it so it wouldn't stop.

The two Christian beach bums kept coming to visit me at the hospital. They were brothers, and they were dating two Christian sisters who were very "prophetic," and they told me that I needed to never go back to that cult and that this accident had happened to get me out of there.

Also, when I was having nightmares, they came and prayed for me outside of the hospital, and the nightmares stopped. I did experience a miraculous recovery.

After a month in reconstructive surgery, I went to rehab, and within a month, the hospital sent me home with a leg brace. My church friends picked me up the day after I got released, and they took me to Magic Mountain, where we were first in line to get on all the rides at the very front since I was in a wheelchair. To this day, I wonder if that's why they took me there in the first place.

Three months later, I was surfing again. I had no emotional trauma and was able to ride my bike up and down the boardwalk. It turned out that I had the two best orthopedic and reconstructive surgery doctors in the county. One of them passed away a month later from a heart attack.

CHAPTER EIGHT
The Shamans

Two different surf bums from a different church offered to take me to this new church they attended, and eventually, the pastor at the new church got caught on camera kissing a male student.

By now, I was fed up with religion, and shortly after, I met my first ex-wife, who is the one I mentioned in chapter 2 of my second Sasquatch story. We had lots of ups and downs; we lived together for several years, and eventually, she moved to another state, and I ended up following her there.

I hated that state at first. There was no beach, it was super cold in the winter, I didn't know anyone, and it looked like an economically depressed state at the time. I ended up marrying my partner, but we divorced a year later.

As I was ready to leave the state, I strongly felt that I was not supposed to go anywhere, and after receiving confirmation in several ways, I decided to stay. I joined a church that soon kicked me out for believing in the supernatural.

I eventually ended up going through a ministry that did prophetic readings similar to psychic readings, and I ended up taking a year-long training in supernatural healing, prophetic readings, dream interpretation, and other things, only to get kicked out again because, according to them, I was too radical.

At this point, I was wondering what the whole purpose of even being in that state was, and that's when I started joining a ton of outdoor groups and started making trips every weekend.

Life took on a whole new meaning in exploring mountains, lakes, and everything around, and I really started to catch on to the outdoor lifestyle the state had to offer. I realized that the people there were really friendly, and this, of course, was years before the nasty influx of California transplants to that state that took place later on. At least at that time, I had finally found some temporary stability.

During those outdoorsy years, I met a friend at the outdoors groups who claimed to be Shamanic or what she referred to as a white witch. I had no idea what she was talking about, but some time after I got kicked out of the last church, she and I felt a strong connection of sorts during a trip. We were laughing a lot, and she felt we needed to connect more.

I didn't know what to think of her Shamanic and witchy claims, but as I asked Spirit, I clearly heard, "This is your destiny."

So, we decided to go to watch a movie and get to know each other, and I biked over to her house. What happened next changed everything.

During the night prior to visiting my new friend. I felt a spiritual excitement I had not felt before. I arrived at her house, and I remembered a scripture that said something along the lines of greeting the house, and if it receives you, your peace will rest upon it, and if it doesn't, leave and shake the dust off your feet.

Well, she had also put a spell over the house where no one could enter unless they had the highest intentions for her and her house.

She welcomed me and gave me a tour of her house. As I entered, I started getting a huge sense that the presence of God was there. I could see in the Spirit as I walked through the house that something in the walls was rearranging spiritually like a Tetris game.

She showed me her bedroom, and I honestly kept getting more and more drunk in the Spirit, and she did, too. We didn't know what was going on as the vibration kept getting higher and higher in her house. It was like a revival meeting was breaking out at the witch's house all of a sudden. We both felt this unspeakable joy.

I had no grid for anything that was happening, and neither did she. All I knew was that the high vibration in the room was awfully familiar, but I had felt it only in the religious environments that they kicked me out of.

I finally made it to her living room, and I told her I sensed a vortex there, and she told me that was where she did her astral travel. I asked Spirit what she was talking about, and all I heard was, "Just go with it and do NOT speak my name." That was super odd for me to hear, so I tried to interpret what she was telling me without judging the difference in word semantics.

Keep in mind that I had no clue that any of this even existed, and I was clearly stepping into unknown territory, but fear was the last thing on my mind. I started getting downloads about her life and sharing them with her, and we both started getting so drunk in the high spiritual energy that showed up that we were almost incoherent.

She then decided we needed to go for a walk towards the movie theater, so we took off. As we were walking, I got more and more spiritual downloads for her, and she started to get energetically free and charged. We got to the point where we were completely drunk in the Spirit, but we had not taken anything nor prayed nor anything to be that way.

We arrived at the downtown area, and we were about two blocks away from the theater when I got a vision of two medieval armies making a truce; as I shared this with her, this super glorious heaviness came over us and overtook us to where we were on the ground laughing hysterically for no reason, and we couldn't even walk.

We literally were acting as if we had smoked a really big joint, but we had taken nothing. People were walking past us as we were laughing, completely fumigated on the floor, and they were acting as if it was completely normal that we could not get off the floor.

Eventually, after lots of struggle, we managed to cross the street and get to the parking lot of the movie theater, but we were too wasted to be able to go in without causing a ruckus.

So we decided to go find a bench and sit down at the park next door, and a lady who was sitting at a bench saw us coming and took off running. After we sat down, it was more than obvious that this wasn't your normal hanging out. My friend started saying, "What is it that I'm not seeing?" repeatedly.

She then asked me if I would allow her to look into me, and I had no clue what she was talking about. I asked Spirit, and I got a resounding "yes," so she put her hand on my chest, rolled her eyes backward, and started convulsing. That was nice, I thought to myself, but we had been laughing so hard that I wasn't threatened by this.

She then came out of her trance and proceeded to tell me that she saw a giant lion of fire and that it was my spirit animal. I again had no clue of what she was talking about, and Spirit told me "Lion of Judah," so I said Yes, I work with a lion. Then she mentioned that she saw how it opened its mouth and out of it came a ball of fire that went right into her, and that the lion had a demeanor of a protector and almost fatherly, but at the same time, a demeanor that you should never cross.

Things got way more intense after that as she started introducing me to all her friends that she had tried to help, and as I would go to her house to meet them, I would ask them not to tell me anything, and I would get the whole download of who they were, what the problem was and what Spirit was saying to them and they got unbelievable breakthroughs in their lives.

It just kept getting more and more intense, and all the gifts and training I had received in the previous years came to life.

I kept asking, "Who are these people?" and I heard something audibly that changed my perspective forever about spiritual people. I audibly heard,

"These are my children; I want them to go with my power."

Mind that in the Christian religion, to be called children of God meant you were of the same religious conviction, but God was telling me otherwise. I never heard that I should try to convert anyone to the Christian religion; I heard simply that God wanted his children (the common spiritual folk) to utilize His Power. That was a first for me.

CHAPTER NINE
The Pastor and the Dragon T-Shirt

During my year of training at a school of supernatural ministry, I experienced a lot of personal attacks coming from the pastor in charge.

His church always had lots of miraculous manifestations, and this fit me quite well at the time. However, the pastor had married a woman very quickly, who later turned out to be the ex-wife of a prominent musician from a very well-known heavy metal band that was very well known for being involved heavily in the very dark side of the occult.

One night, Spirit had me write down a very detailed prophetic message, which was a warning to the pastor. I delivered it to him and his wife in private. The message was a stern warning saying that he was at a crossroads and that he must give up control. If he gave up control, his church would take new, amazing heights and would explode in more signs and wonders, but if he didn't give up control, his church would fall apart.

After delivering the word, the pastor and his new wife told me that I could not graduate unless I recanted that word. I asked Spirit what to do, and I was told to graduate, so I recanted the word to be able to finish my school. The church fell apart in one day, the very weekend that I graduated, and to this day, it never went back to what it used to be.

Later, I found out that many people had come to the pastor with the exact same message, and he kicked them all out of the church, which amounted to about thirty families, including visitors who had all received and delivered the same exact message to the pastor and his wife.

By now, I was quite unsettled about churches in general, and this was during a time when I had just finished my dream interpretation training, and I was going to help at a yearly local metaphysical fair with a Christian group that did prophetic readings and dream interpretation.

I kept getting strong, powerful messages of encouragement for people who came for readings from the metaphysical and energy healing community, and the leaders of my Christian group did not like my intensity, even though the messages I got for the people were life-changing.

I remember that when I was on my way to the event, I had seen a T-shirt at a second-hand store that had a Chinese dragon imprint. The T-shirt really called me, but I wasn't used to esoteric symbols, so I left the store only to be pulled back to the store to buy it and wear it for the event.

I had not realized until now that the dragon was also a catalyst for my spiritual evolution. I was about to throw the T-shirt away while decluttering after I had written this book years later and was reminded of that event, so I kept the shirt and had to go back to add this section to the book as well.

CHAPTER TEN
The Glory Days

At this point, it was more than clear that I was making a quantum leap into uncharted territory—at least for me. It felt like a never-ending adventure.

My spiritual experiences were no longer happening at church (since I had stopped going) but instead at the least expected places. Soon, I started meeting other spiritual people who were not connected to my shamanic friend.

My shaman friend later took off permanently to travel the world.

Later, I was invited by my friend Alex, who would eventually become my student in traditional Spanish sword fighting, to a potluck, where I suddenly started doing spiritual readings for a bunch of people.

One lady, in particular, was very interested in getting to know Alex and me because we spoke Spanish, and she had spent time in South America doing shamanic work.

When she realized I was able to do spiritual readings, she wanted to book some time with me. So, we met at a coffee shop later in the week. It all felt so normal to me—like it was all meant to happen.

I was eager to channel whatever information I got from God for this lady, and not surprisingly, it all resonated with her on such a deep level that she later said she could have worked six months on the issue she inquired about, and in just 20 minutes of us casually hanging out, she got the answers she desperately needed. I was just thrilled that I was hearing correctly and able to make a difference.

I remember telling her that she was a person of spiritual influence in her community and that there was a specific group of people only she could reach. That she was going to be used to change people's lives in ways no one else could.

That she was a leader of sorts and that her calling was a complete confirmation of everything she had heard and received in her earlier years.

She later told me she wanted to show me the influence she had in the community and invited me to an event she had been led to organize regarding the end of the Mayan calendar in 2012. Things were about to get really interesting.

For the first time in my life, I felt connected to a spiritual group of people that didn't make me feel like an outsider looking in.

Finally, the day came for the great Mayan calendar event. We met at a house that was absolutely unbelievable—there were so many spiritual people attending.

There were ceremonies of all sorts, music playing, people coming in and out, didgeridoo music, food being shared, and many other shenanigans and activities—spiritual activations, teachings—and what Spirit told me to do was to hold space in God's presence for the event. That's what I did. I met the most amazing leaders in this incredible community that was just starting to take shape, and I was given many downloads, prayers, and things to do that caused many miracles to be unleashed.

The event lasted for several days across different locations, and the connections and experiences would take a lifetime to write. I was finally home, in a sense—connected, spiritually thriving, and able to make a difference in people's lives.

We all had something to contribute, and the dynamics were really healthy and powerful. It was beyond a dream come true— a spiritual utopia of sorts. Something I had never imagined. This was, for me, the beginning of a lifetime journey in the spiritual realm.

My connection with Christ has never been replaced. It has evolved into a more understanding, open, and compassionate way of being toward people of different ideological convictions that point to spirituality. My perspective has definitely shifted for the better, as I see that true spirituality is much different from how we have been conditioned. Yet, many people have it right, and many people have it backward—but it's not for anyone to judge as we shift and evolve on a daily basis.

I've noticed that many people end up leaving religion to embark on a spiritual journey of their own, creating a separation between their former church days and their current path, and they adopt an "us and them" mentality. In reality, there is no separation. Both experiences have their place and time, and both are cornerstones of our growth.

What I've noticed is that when I began to integrate both experiences, I became more whole, and I can go anywhere I'm called to be without inner conflict or self-imposed labels to define my identity.

I have learned to listen to different perspectives and receive knowledge, and many times, help and insight from precious humans who stood with me in the trenches of life. I've been able to do the same for others and share my insights, helping as I receive direction from Source—and it always works out beautifully.

God/Spirit/Source is not a religion or a dogma—it's a personal experience to be had.

There is wisdom and knowledge in all paths, and we shouldn't throw out the baby with the bathwater. We are all evolving, and we shouldn't limit what we can benefit from. We can learn from all sources neutrally and receive the messages that come to edify, build, and encourage us.

Everyone can have antagonistic views toward other spiritual

convictions—or even people within their own circles. It's human nature to become guarded toward what is different and makes us uncomfortable. And yes, there are spiritual energies everywhere—even within us—that we need to be aware of, but our spiritual growth stands on the other side, waiting for us to take a step.

CHAPTER ELEVEN
Chaos and Rebirth

As this spiritual vortex, I was in continued to unfold, I kept getting consistent assignments to go to different places and channels for specific people, and whatever I was given to do at the last minute, I did gladly.

I never knew what would happen next. I never turned my spiritual gifts into a business, and I was happy to just make a difference in people's lives.

For some reason, I thought that if there were no miracles, I was not connected to the source, and there were always a lot of miracles, but eventually, I realized that there are different seasons for everything and that our connection to the source lies within ourselves and that our spiritual experience should evolve and not be stagnant in any given phase.

Sometimes, we are called to help and heal others; sometimes, we are called to rest, move to places, and so on.

People kept contacting me for help, and they were always coming in and out of my house. At the same time, Spirit told me to "Start Sword fighting."

I had no idea what that would look like for me, so I contacted a historical renaissance group that met only a few blocks away from my house on Saturdays, and my sword fighting journey began. Eventually, I figured out that Spain had the most advanced treatise on medieval sword fighting, but no one in the group knew about it, so I dug out the treaties written in old Spanish and started my own group.

I was quite busy between spiritual work, sword-fighting, and outdoor trips, and life was really good. I'm a person who craves variety, so I picked up as many hobbies as I could and stored gear for them, but eventually, I realized that it was best to have a few hobbies and become good at them. I loved this period of my life. There were years when I only stayed home 2 weekends out of the whole year because I was doing so many outdoor trips and activities.

I had become quite popular in the spiritual community. There were many invites to all sorts of events, circles, and community shenanigans.

One day, I was invited to the inauguration of a community healing center, and a beautiful woman walked in whom I had not seen before, and she later became my wife.

Things moved very fast between us. I had seen her in many visions before, and she had seen me as well, so when we met, we recognized each other.

She had asked some of my friends who I was and decided to talk to me, and it was game over. We met several times after that, and she moved in quickly with me, along with her son, her 12 cats, and her dog. She had had a very sad past and was rebuilding her life, having moved from another state.

Up to this point, I had bought a house and was living with my best friend, David. We had had many adventures together where he witnessed some amazing energy work and healings that I was led to do in the community and at festivals. He was like my little brother from Puerto Rico, and we always had a great time together, and he complimented me very well.

At some point, while I was at work about to take my lunch, Spirit dragged me to a second-hand store where I purchased a didgeridoo. I instinctively figured out how to play it, and this opened even more doors to events and circles as I learned how to use it for healing work. David and I met on a rock-climbing trip with other friends, and I had taken my didgeridoo with me and played by the fire under the stars before our big multi-pitch climb.

From that point, we became almost inseparable. We took a trip to the coast to attend a didgeridoo festival, and he witnessed me swatting a fairy as it came up on my face and many other supernatural things as well. I mentioned some of this in my chapter about the Bosnian pyramid.

As my relationship with my new girlfriend progressed, we started partying almost every night. David also met a girl from Oregon, and neither he nor I smoked or drank at that time, but when we met these two girls, we started smoking weed with them every night.

I was never addicted to anything, and David had stopped drinking alcohol, but he was never an alcoholic. As days went by and I started losing sleep, the partying did not slow down, and I was getting irritable.

Both my girlfriend and his girlfriend were lifetime weed smokers, and David and I were not used to this.

He had more of an addictive personality, and he took smoking on and became a pro. I just couldn't get into it as much, but my girl was doing it all the time. I also noticed that she liked privacy, and David and I were social and spiritual butterflies, and things started changing.

My girl insisted on getting married, and the beautiful wedding took place at a park for all to witness. We chose medieval and mystic outfits and swords, of course.

There was a Christian, a witch, and a shaman as our wedding priests and priestesses. It almost sounded like a Mexican joke, and I had always been able to build bridges between people of different beliefs, and this was no exception.

3 divorces later with the same girl, I ended up in a deep depression. The community was gone. David was gone, and the magic was gone. I kept the house, and she moved to a different state, and I was not the same person anymore. Neither was she. It was very sad.

So far, I have become internationally recognized in Europe as a Spanish

Sword fighting instructor, and this practice kept me sane and active through all the mess. Then COVID came, and I got sick, and I almost died. When I finally started recovering, my good friend and boss got sick with COVID, and he passed away 3 weeks later.

He was in his early thirties and left 4 kids and a wife. I had worked for a larger roofing company before as a salesperson, and he found out that they were stealing my wages and hired me as a salesperson. We were doing really well. He was such an amazing human being, and when I got sick, he even did my work and paid me.

His friend, who is also amazing, bought the business and became a really dear friend to me. I continued to work for the company, but I had to take a break, so I went to travel through Spain for three months. COVID had taken my spiritual sensitivity away; I felt disconnected, sad, and dry, and I needed a hard reset.

CHAPTER TWELVE
The Spanish Dagger

My first Sword fighting event occurred at a castle in a Spanish town called Montilla in the southern region of Andalucia. It was a dream come true.

I wanted to see how well I had figured out this Spanish martial art, and to my surprise, I did way better than I thought. Verdadera Destreza is the name of the Spanish martial art that deals with rapier sword combat of the 15th and 16th centuries, and it originated in medieval Spain. Verdadera Destreza means True Dexterity, and unlike modern fencing, where the attacks are linear, there is no control over the opponent's sword, and whoever hits first wins.

Verdadera Destreza uses circles and angles as applied geometry to control and create counterattacks and disarms at the right moment, and it is based on footwork distance management and different sciences such as geometry, physics, and mathematics.

I always taught it to my students as a non-competitive art, with emphasis on correct technique and application. It had been almost 10 years since I started deciphering the art and practicing at the park with my students.

We basically figured out the whole martial arts from scratch, and when the masters from Spain saw our work, they could not believe we learned on our own.

I had booked my trip for 2 months to Spain, but I ended up staying for 3. I visited sword schools and cities all over Spain, such as Malaga, Montilla, Cordoba, Granada, Valencia, Castellón, Barcelona, San Sebastián in the basque country, Oviedo in Asturias, Madrid, Toledo, The Canary Islands, and then I flew to Kiev, Ukraine and left for Greece, back to Malaga and arrived home 2 weeks before they bombed the airport in Kiev, Ukraine.

I met amazing people in Spain, and I learned that the history we have been taught in the American continent about Spain and the origins of America is a complete British and French-originated lie.

I learned that Spain did not have colonies but Viceroyalties and that the Viceroyalty of New Spain covered from Alaska, western Canada to Louisiana and met with the region of Peru in the south where the Viceroyalty of Peru was located.

I learned that Queen Isabel had strictly prohibited slavery of the natives and that they were protected under the laws of Indies and the laws of Burgos, which were the predecessors of the human rights laws we have today, and that the concept of racial inequality was never a Spanish concept but a British concept and the natives were considered equal subjects to the Spanish Crown and conserved their lands and had ranks equal to the Spanish rulers since they were part of the same Spanish empire and that Moctezuma from now Mexico and Atahualpa from Peru were considered kings of Spain and their statues remain among all the statues of the kings of Spain today at the royal palace in Madrid.

I learned that the United States, under the guise of Canadian companies, extracts more gold out of Mexico per year than Spain did through its whole empire and that out of all the gold extracted by Spain, only the Royal 5th, or a fifth part went to Castilla (which was the name the Spanish kingdom at the time

) and it was the tax that everyone paid, and the rest was invested in the first 25 all-inclusive universities built for the natives and Spanish alike throughout the whole American continent. Also, I learned that the first Asian university was built by Spain, the University of Manila, Philippines, centuries before Anglo and racially exclusive Harvard and Yale universities were ever built or allowed a so-called colored man to attend.

The gold extracted by Spain was also invested in infrastructure, hospitals, cities, and towns as Spain duplicated and invested in its culture and did not erase native culture.

I learned that Spanish is the first language with a grammatical record in Europe and that the native languages were also learned by Spanish priests, criticized and taught in schools to the natives in the Americas to preserve their culture being Nahuatl, the second language after Spanish to have been grammatically structured before any other language in Europe.

I also learned that the natives in North America had a different culture from the ones in the south and that cultural integration was the primary goal of Castilla (New Spain), but it was more difficult to integrate them in the north than in the south.

I also learned that there was no such thing as an Aztec empire, that the region that the Aztecs occupied was very small, that they migrated from the north, and that they did not build the pyramids but found them.

Also, I was surprised to find out that Mexico did not exist as a country at the arrival of Spain. It was land that was inhabited by territories where different ancient tribes dwelled, and when it became large, Viceroyalties at the gradual arrival of Spain and Mexico only became a nation after the wars of independence from 1810-1820.

The Aztecs were the first culture to carry out a cannibalistic genocide in the region they invaded, and it was carried out through their rituals, which happened once a month in the 13 months of the Aztec calendar that by the time Spain reached that area, the local tribes such as the Tlaxcaltecas and others, were ready to eradicate the Aztecs and 30,000 natives assisted in ending the Aztec oppression with the alliance of less than 1000 Spanish soldiers.

I also learned that the native genocide that occurred in America by Europeans was carried by the British and not Spain, as Spain had no concept of racism like the British did, and there were strict laws (Laws of Burgos and of Indies) against enslaving natives which were considered Spanish citizens of equal or in many cases, higher rank than peninsular Spaniards.

Spain had mestizaje, which was the mixing of cultures through marriages, and Spain was the only country that circumnavigated the whole globe, establishing the largest empire in history. The original discovery records in Australia were Spanish, and it was originally named Australia del Espíritu Santo and the Philippines was also originally a Spanish Viceroyalty.

I also learned that the term Latino is completely incorrect as Latinos are from Rome, Romania, and France since they inherited ancient Latin directly from Rome, and Spanish America inherited ancient Castilian from Castilla, now called España.

French and the British were never able to overcome Spain on the battlefield. Their goal was to erase the history of Spain and rewrite a complete historical fallacy to control the territories and people through propaganda, political infiltration, and historical deceit.

This really opened my eyes to the magnitude of the many fabrications designed to control our perception and make us fit into a reality that others think we should fit into.

My point is that when I think about how historical information is manipulated and obscured, there is no wonder why the information about beings like the Sasquatch or ancient discoveries always appears as a myth or is completely hidden or ridiculed.

We are in the midst of a war on information, and it's our duty to dig deeper into all subjects and question everything. Unfortunately, in many cases, the information is not even available.

It was a fascinating and eye-opening trip but very tiring as I was not only traveling but also sword fighting at many places, and this took a toll on my strength coming back home.

CHAPTER THIRTEEN
The Dark Night of the Soul

As soon as I got back home from Spain, I fell into a deep depression again. I could barely work, and I stayed in bed for months. I was renting the rooms to roommates and running up my credit cards. I had no strength and no will to do anything.

As amazing as my trip was, I was still grieving my divorce, and I was stuck in a mental rut about what I could have done better. I had met many women through my trip to Spain, but I still couldn't solve the emotional puzzle that my divorce from my ex left imprinted in my soul.

I kept feeling a nudge that I needed to sell the house, which reminded me of her every day, and I felt like I needed to move altogether to a different state. I spent the next 2 years depressed and wondering if I should sell the house or not.

I started selling my stuff and tried doing roofing sales here and there when I had the energy to stay afloat. The roofing business depended on me for sales, but I just could not work up the mindset to be able to do it consistently.

I had started attending a church and helping at the food pantry to get food and spiritual support, and it was becoming a life-and-death situation for me as I didn't have much will to live. Other people tried to help me, but I just couldn't snap out of the funk.

My really good girlfriend continued to check up on me. We had met at the Brazilian cult years prior, and after recovering from my accident, I went and got her out of it, and we stayed friends to this day. She recommended me to have a spiritual reading session with someone she knew that could help me.

I had no more spiritual juice left in me, and I was not even a shadow of my former spiritual self. She was also the one who checked on me when I was dying of COVID, and she sent me the medication I needed to get better and basically saved my life. I agreed to contact the person she recommended me to do a reading with, and the reading was life-changing.

It completely gave me the perspective that I needed to make the decision to sell the house, and once I got the process started, the house sold very quickly.

The person who did my reading mentioned to me that I was going through a spiritual quantum reset from all the battles I had gone through in my life, and he spoke about a spiritual and financial restoration season coming in the near future.

Once the house was sold, I entered a vortex of synchronicities that led me to move to a different state and start recovering. My strength started coming back, my spiritual connection became more tangible again, and all things started lining up; I found a job and a perfect place to live and started getting spiritually re-activated once again.

The house that I found was magical; it sat at the edge of a nature reserve for birds of prey with amazing views from the balcony, no neighbors, and a hot tub, and it was perfect for one person. I started exploring the outdoors more and more and getting back to normal. This is when I started noticing the Sasquatch structures everywhere I went.

The house is located in the Pacific Northwest, and the outdoor access and the amount of things to do is absolutely unreal. I became aware of the intensity and density of the many different energies of the new region.

I started doing roofing sales again and getting into downhill mountain biking and camping. I even bought a surfboard and wetsuit and started making trips to the coast.

My strength was back, and I felt more settled and less volatile. I had already given up on the idea that I would ever surf again. It took all the faith I had to make this move out of state, and I started getting messages of reassurance at every step. Once I sold the house and moved, everything started to become magical once again.

CHAPTER FOURTEEN
The Dragon and the Flute of Mount Shasta

I attended a didgeridoo festival during the summer that takes place in the Pacific Northwest and spent a few days camping and enjoying the shows.

One afternoon during this event, I sat down at my camp spot in the meadows, and all of a sudden, I had a strong vision of a dragon that shook me quite a bit. It was powerful and beautiful, but I had no clue what it all meant.

As I worked my way to the community area where the stage was. I found a table that had some stones on display, and I started hanging onto them for dear life as I really needed to ground my body from the vision that I had.

A lady came asking if I was ok, and I mentioned to her what I had seen. She mysteriously looked into my eyes intently and said to me, yes, the dragon will continue to appear to you until you become one.

She told me she was a dragon lady herself. I absolutely had no clue what she was talking about, and I noticed that where the stones that I was hanging onto were, there was a stuffed animal in the shape of a baby dragon.

Then another lady came, and she asked me if I was ok. I mentioned to her about the vision I had and about the lady dragon at the table that I had just been talking with, and she told me she was also a lady dragon herself, and I asked what that meant.

I knew there was a revelation for me to hear, and I needed all the perspective I could get. She told me that she was born in the year of the dragon and that one of her purposes in life was to tame down her tongue and energy so that she would not hurt other people, but she would instead build them and encourage them.

Later during the summer, I was planning another outdoor trip, and a friend reached out to ask me if I would be attending an annual Sasquatch event where we had met, since my plans for that weekend didn't materialize, I headed over to Mount Shasta where the event was taking place.

This was the same event I had attended a few years back, and there were some familiar faces. One lady who knew me told me that she wanted to introduce me to a Russian girlfriend of hers. Later, as we were drumming by the fire, I started playing my didgeridoo, and the night lit up with sound and laughter. The Russian lady came, and we started a conversation, and quickly, our connection became romantic. We met several times in Mount Shasta as this was the middle point between where we lived.

During my last trip to Shasta, I stopped at a store, and this giant drone flute caught my attention, but the price tag of $345 was not in my plans. I played it at the store, and I played another smaller flute as well. I noticed how the atmosphere got much brighter when I played.

Both flutes were about the same price, but I put them back and found a small red stone dragon head, and I bought it for $6.

I walked out of the store and went to another crystal store next door and played their didgeridoo for a while. As I left, I went back past the store that sold the flutes, and Spirit told me to sit down at some small steps outside. I sat down, and I was still thinking about buying the flute, but I wanted to feel into it for a moment, so I got on my phone looking for a place to buy a smoothie so I could go think about whether or not to buy the flute.

As I was looking down at my phone, a complete stranger walked out of the store and put the big flute between my phone and my face. I saw it and looked up at him, and he said with this beautiful, knowing smile, "For you, brother." I grabbed the flute in complete amazement and said, almost screaming in disbelief, "Are you serious!!??"

I looked down to see the massive flute in my hands as I was taking a huge breath in amazement, and my heart was racing and pounding like crazy. When I looked back up, the stranger had walked away without looking back, but I could tell he had a big smile on his face. I absolutely had no words, and I started crying.

As I was pondering this, a group of people from Brazil pulled up in a van and parked right behind me, and a lady saw that I was sitting there holding this massive flute, and she came and sat next to me and said, "I was asking the Universe to let me hear someone play the flute this morning."

I just couldn't believe what was unfolding right before me, and I started telling the lady what had just happened a minute earlier and how I got the flute.

The timing was unbelievable.

Some other people heard me saying this, and they stopped by and wanted to hear it as well, so I started playing, and it was just the most powerful, amazing sound…. I was choking, crying, and playing all at the same time.

I don't have words to describe it.

I wanted to show my new friend how the didgeridoo sounded as well, and we headed next door to the crystal shop. We walked to the back where the didgeridoo was, and I shared my story about the dragon of my childhood and how I had just bought a small dragon head just before the stranger gave me the flute. It was too much coincidence.

I played the didgeridoo for her, and she went into a deep meditation. Then she pointed at the didgeridoo I was playing and mentioned that she noticed that it had a blue Dragon engraved on it, and she said that I should buy it. The didgeridoo actually belonged to the owner, and it was an icon of that store in Shasta for many years, and it was not for sale.

She insisted on talking to the manager as if it was a done deal that I should buy it, and I'm sure she would have bought it for me, but instead, she ended up getting in an argument with the ladies at the front desk who explained to her that if Spirit told them to give it to someone, they absolutely would and they took my phone number but my friend kept insisting, and the subject of the dragon came up somehow.

One of the ladies there said something very significant, which I had to write down. She said: "The message of the dragon is to stop being the warrior to be able to hold the fire for the people."

Finally, my friend and I gave up on the didgeridoo and left the store and went to the headwaters to play the flute and do a blessing around the area. When we got there, she shared with me that she was a temple follower of Paramahansa Yogananda and explained to me his life and doctrine and how this man traveled to bring yoga to the United States.

She shared how this man taught doctrines of inner peace and meditation, how he was rejected and mistreated in America, and how he would put himself in abusive situations to practice his teachings, which were very similar to the message of the dragon at the store earlier so I noticed the pattern.

She then gave me a picture of Paramahansa Yogananda and mentioned to me that she had offered it to the lady at the didgeridoo shop who also went to the same temple as my friend, but the other lady there kept her from receiving it. It seemed to be a precious item for them, and I gave her a piece of Moldevite in exchange, and the peaceful message of the dragon and of Paramahansa Yogananda became clear.

We had a beautiful ceremony, playing and meditating by the headwaters, and later, we went to have pizza and to meet with her group and parted ways.

Later, I realized that the dragon had been appearing to me to help me transition out of strife, trauma, and fear from my past and into peaceful power and self-control, and the message of the dragon at the store and the life of Paramahansa Yogananda made more sense than ever.

Later, I realized that if Spirit brings us to a realization, Spirit will also help us embody and integrate that realization so we can become the message, and the same message can come in different forms and that no religion nor dogma owns the right to what Spirit wants to convey to people.

CHAPTER FIFTEEN
Europe, Here We Go

It had been almost three years since my trip to Spain, and I was hoping to make another trip after I sold my house.

After settling at my new place, I started camping and exploring my new state and surroundings.

I kept finding and documenting more and more Sasquatch structures, and after a few months, I had hundreds of recorded structures, footprints, and locations.

It seemed like every time I went camping, I found structures. I started hanging out and camping with my Native American friend, who now lived in the same state as I did and who had an ongoing relationship with a Sasquatch clan.

Her son also has an ongoing relationship with these beings, and every time she and I camped together, the Sasquatch came to us. We could hear them, we could see them in some instances, and we could feel them.

After my last trip to Shasta, things fell apart between my Russian girlfriend and me, and I felt it was time to schedule my flight to Europe as winter was coming and my work was seasonal. The date came all too quickly, and I was not even in the traveling mindset. I packed lightly and arrived in Sevilla the next day.

I knew I was going to be connected with the right people, but I didn't know it would happen right away. As I arrived at the first hostel, I noticed a girl who had been sitting all day on her bunk bed. She had not eaten all day, and Spirit told me to invite her to get a bite to eat.

As we were walking, we both felt an immediate connection, and I asked her what her story was.

She said it was complicated—that she wasn't traveling for pleasure, didn't have a home, and was from Iran—so I didn't insist on asking further. But when we sat down at a pizza parlor, Spirit gave me a download synopsis of her life. I told her what I was getting, and she completely agreed.

She was an energy worker and psychologist who was working on a lifetime project and would only do as Spirit instructed her to do. After the death of her husband, her spiritual understanding drove her to live the way she was living, and it had been a hard road.

What are the chances that the first person I met in Europe was a spiritual person?

After a few lovely days visiting Sevilla with her, it was time for me to start moving along the coast toward Portugal.

I visited the town of Huelva on the way. I wanted to get to Lagos, Portugal, to have some quiet time because I had been led to bring a book called Nonviolent Communication, which I felt was part of walking out the message of the dragon and of Paramahansa Yogananda.

I spent a few days in Lagos, Portugal, enjoying the quiet and gorgeous beaches of the Algarve, biking to different places, eating sushi, reading my book, soaking up the message it contained, and enjoying the sun and the views. I was really proud of myself when I finished reading it.

I felt like a veil had been lifted from my eyes, and I could clearly see the life lessons of this precious book. My life was changed forever… or so I thought.

I later took off toward Lisbon, and when I arrived, I just did not like what I saw. I arrived at my hostel, and I might as well have arrived in Istanbul, Algeria, or back at the store where I used to work.

The place seemed very dirty and unkempt. There was graffiti everywhere, and this just did not resemble the Lisbon I had visited years ago.

Literally, a few minutes after I arrived, there was a riot at the very corner where I checked in at the hostel. There were police in riot gear everywhere, and the whole city was paralyzed by the diversion of the heavy Christmas traffic because of the riots.

I decided to go for a walk, away from the chaos, and eventually made it to downtown Lisbon—only to get in a fight with two Black men after they almost ran me over and cursed at me while I was crossing the street.

I had a gash on my hand that was going to require stitches from hitting their taillights, and my hand was bleeding. All of a sudden, I realized that there was more to just reading a book and feeling good about it.

As I walked away, I found a red hiking scarf on the ground, and since it was clean, I wrapped it around my bloody hand and headed back to the nasty hostel. It was like the Mad Max movie—Euro version 2.0. I arrived late at the hostel, bloody and tired, but I did manage to take some awesome night pictures on the way back.

The next day, I had to do something about my wounds, so I decided I didn't want to go to the hospital. I remembered that super glue was invented to close up the wounds of soldiers in Vietnam, so I did what Rambo would do: I got some Neosporin, some super glue, and some bandages.

I decided I wasn't enjoying this place much, but I still checked out the city for another day and took the bus to downtown Lisbon again. It was very crowded and dirty since it was just before Christmas, but I did manage to have a good time and relax.

I then found, on Google Maps, a town called Sintra, about an hour away by train, that caught my attention. I booked a room there and took the train out of Lisbon.

As I pondered what had happened in Lisbon, I decided that I wasn't going to have a bad attitude about it and that I couldn't get mad at those men—because the whole incident could have been avoided if I had remembered everything I read in that stupid book, and if I hadn't turned around and yelled back at them through their window as they almost ran me over. I had already almost lost a leg in my previous accident with someone similar, so their attitude really irritated me.

By the time I noticed, it was too late, and they were charging at me like the evil African albino monk from Epic Movie. I remember, between punches, kicks, and blows, I was thinking to myself in my heart that I really wanted to live the essence of that book.

I started practicing gratitude for the lessons and for everything I could think of, and I took a good laugh at myself and at the ridiculous situations, circumstances, and events.

As I became grateful, I didn't realize that this decision had marked a cornerstone in the beginning of my new spiritual expansion as the trip evolved.

The lesson was all about overcoming conflict.

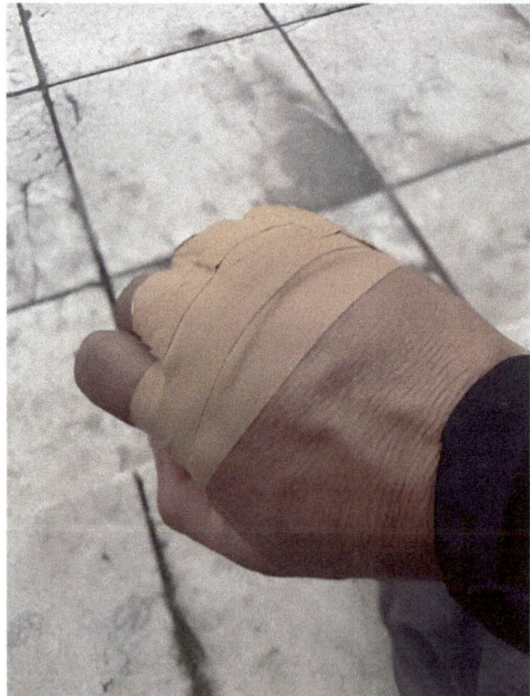

CHAPTER SIXTEEN
Sasquatch in Portugal

As I arrived in colorful Sintra, Portugal, there was a tour moped parked next to the train station, and it had pictures of the local castles.

As I was reading the description, I asked the girl at the wheel the cost of the ride. It was steep, but I felt I should take it.

She was a quick thinker and fun and lively, and as she was sharing about the castles during the ride, I also commented that I did Sasquatch research and mentioned details about the structures and the ways the Sasquatch make themselves known to people in the forests. She was very interested and mentioned to me that she had felt some weird vibes while hiking in a section of the local forest.

She tried to stop and get gas, and the gas stations were being serviced; it was an adventure doing the tour with her while she was running out of gas, but we made it, and she then invited me to go have soup at a shop where she always stops to take a break.

I felt I needed to pay for her lunch and still give her a tip even though she was charging a lot and the tour bus only cost€13. As we were sitting on the sunny benches outside, I channeled a beautiful message of an encouraging word for her, and she was extremely receptive and teary-eyed about it.

Normally, as a tour guide, she never took people anywhere past the actual tour, but we were having such a good conversation that she felt she wanted to share with me about her life and work, and we became friends.

She was from Canada, and she had a little daughter and bought the moped to support herself and the baby by doing tours.

She told me she wanted to take me to the forest, where she always felt weird sensations while hiking, and she gave me tons of local tips about the area. We exchanged numbers and set up a time for her to pick me up the next day in her car to go to the forest. She finally gave me a ride to the historical area where my hostel was located.

After settling in, another traveler at the hostel asked me what happened to my hand. I told her the story of what happened in Lisbon, and she was really puzzled that something like this would happen in Portugal.

Later, I realized that I saw Portugal through the lens of fear and trauma that I had lived at the store, and after paying attention to the people who lived there, I noticed that they were very relaxed and friendly as a culture, and I realized that I had created that whole situation.

The riots were not riots but demonstrations against weather manipulation, and they were peaceful. This realization gave me insight and allowed me to start shifting my reality by becoming more self-aware, and it took me one solid step further into my healing.

I went to visit a castle called Qunta De Regaliera that really caught my attention online, and it was the reason I was drawn to go to Sintra.

My friend mentioned that it was an amazing mystical place built by the Masons and Knights Templar, and it was made for initiations into their magical orders.

This place did not disappoint at all, and looking back, I can say that it blows out of the water any other castle I have ever seen in Europe (aside from La Sagrada Familia in Barcelona).

It is not only the castle that is so amazing, but the grounds surrounding it have extremely mystical passages, meditation areas in the forest, and a 9-level spiral ceremonial downward staircase made of stone representing the 9 levels the templars descended blindfolded into the underworld that led to a tunnel system and mystical fountains covered in moss and ferns, underground wet cave labyrinths, ceremonial areas and meditation sitting places among green lush forest and massive rocks with green mossy waters with rocky steps that went into tunnels, devil and dragon sculptures, the sigil of Lucifer by a big throne made of granite with giant pots on both sides of the stone throne that had carved devils and horned goats.

It was Pagan to the core without any apologies and had nothing catholic nor religious in it, and it was nothing less than magical and capable of making Harry Potter extremely envious.

It almost felt like you could run into Pan, the mystical horned Satyr, at any moment. I could literally spend all day there, and I wanted to spend the night there in a cave while everyone was gone.

I was happy to do some grid work at the castle and play my flute in the caves to invert the energies from the rituals that once had taken place there. The energy was not that heavy anymore as this place had become a very popular tourist attraction, and it had more positive energy by now.

The next day, my guide friend picked me up in her tiny but cool car. She gave me all the ins and outs of what to visit as my private tour guide, but this time, she didn't charge me, and we arrived at the top of the ridge in the forest where there was a catholic convent and a 360-degree view of the coastal and mountain area.

As we approached the forest, we immediately felt the presence of the forest people (The Sasquatch). We also felt the hairs on our necks stand up, and before entering the forest, I took out my flute and started playing and greeting them in light language.

As soon as we entered the forest, I noticed structures all around, and we started examining them; I started showing my friend how they were built and how they could not have been built by humans without having machinery and without tearing up the flooring of the forest, which was intact.

I took many pictures, and when I started shooting a video of one of the structures, we both heard a long howl that almost sounded like an ambulance right on the other side of the trees. It was a single long howl, but it was not an ambulance because there were no roads there, and it made that sound once and for a long time, and then it stopped and got caught on the video.

It came from one static place behind the trees, and it was definitely not an ambulance, as ambulances move quickly and keep going and going as they drive away. Somehow, we didn't fully notice it, but later, I noticed it when I replayed the video.

She then took me to some megalithic structures, and we had something to eat there. We found numerous structures similar to small huts everywhere, and I was able to find them in Vienna, Austria, later on as well.

Later, we drove to the town of Cascais, where she lived by the coast, and there were many surf spots, and the city was lovely. She gave tons of tips about what to do, dropped me off, and told me how to get back to Sintra. I had a chance to rent a bike to visit the town and experience this beautiful part of Portugal.

CHAPTER SEVENTEEN
The Sasquatch of Northern Spain

It was finally time to leave Sintra and start traveling North.

I pondered about visiting Nazaré where the giant waves are on the Portugal coast, but it was hard to get there, and I had promised my Swordfighting student Joseph that I would visit him in Vienna as he had moved there a year prior, so I took the bus to Porto, the second largest city in Portugal and bought an airplane ticket from there to Amsterdam.

The app that I used made a mistake, and I ended up booking my flight for a month later instead of that week as I had planned. I had to make a decision when I was at the airport and realized the mistake of staying in Porto and exploring it, then traveling around for a month and returning to Porto to fly to Amsterdam.

I had an amazing time in Porto. By now, I was catching onto the Portuguése vibe and culture, and I found it lovely. I was past the trauma of Lisbon and was flowing in gratitude every day, even through the setbacks of my flight.

I found the most amazing all-you-can-eat sushi restaurant, biked all over town, and made it to the beach on the south side of the river to watch the waves on a rainy afternoon.

Eventually, I decided that I still needed to explore the northwestern and central-western portions of Spain that I had not seen yet, so I took a bus to Santiago de Compostela in Galicia, Spain.

I had just picked it on the map and didn't realize that this was the iconic town where the Camino de Santiago pilgrimage route culminates, starting somewhere in France.

What a feeling and what a place!! I explored for the first night after checking in, and the following day, I met a girl from Italy who was sitting in the lounge area of the hostel and who had spent 2 months hiking the Camino. It was another perfect divine connection about to unfold.

As we started talking and sharing our experiences, I mentioned finding Sasquatch in Portugal and about my experiences in the US as well. I was amazed at how open she was as well to hear about this. Of course, she was waking up spiritually as her experiences during her pilgrimage opened her eyes in many ways.

She mentioned that she worked for a yacht crew and that she had been fired for refusing to take verbal abuse by a passenger.

I had found on the map a hiking area called the Mystical Forest, where there were many statues hidden around by the trails of goblins, mermaids, and mythical creatures nearby, and she wanted to join me as I had been telling her about the Sasquatch, but she was feeling a bit sick from something she ate so I gave her an oregano oil pill, and she felt better, and we took off to see the place.

It was nice hiking with someone who could keep a good pace, and we made it to the trailhead quickly.

This place felt very Squatchy as well although the trees were thinner and it had different vegetation than Sintra. We soon found the iconic X structures made of upside-down trees, and I was amazed at how easily we were led to them.

We found footprints as well, and I also took many pictures during our hike. It was rainy, but we had umbrellas, and we hiked until we almost saw all of the sculptures. We found lots of Sasquatch structures until it got too dark to continue.

We then returned to town and decided to go eat. We were craving hamburgers, and she found an excellent place with organic meat, and our visit was lovely.

The following day, I explored more of the city and found out there was another hiking area where there were some ancient glyphs on the opposite side of town, but she had already left town, so I hiked there alone.

As I entered the forest, I had a feeling I was going to find something, and I was right. About half an hour into my hike, I noticed to my left two trees that had been broken in the same direction, and they were too big for it to be wind.

As I explored the area, I found some massive fresh footprints on the trail, so I opened another portal and started playing my flute. It was a very clean forest and well taken care of. All the surrounding trees were perfectly standing upright except for those two broken trees, and this was not a wind area at all.

I eventually found the ancient glyphs on a rock, took a break, ate and drank water, and caught the bus back to town. I was blown away at how easily I was finding Sasquatch structures all over the place.

From Santiago, I decided to head to La Coruña on the northern coast of Spain. The culture and vibe in Spain is a complete opposite than in Portugal. It is way more intense, louder, and more festive.

La Coruña is a very well-developed coastal city, very beautiful, modern, and very efficient. Definitely a city best explored on a bicycle, and they have excellent bike lanes and trails everywhere.

There were many surfing spots and megaliths along the beaches, and they have the iconic Torre de Hercules. Which I believe worked as an ancient Roman lighthouse. After a few days, I decided to travel to another coastal town with more forests called Ferrol, and that's where things got interesting.

My Native American friend had told me that the forest people wanted a specific Spanish fruit that I could not find at stores. They showed it to her in a vision, and she described it to me.

I went to the local stores as I was preparing for my hike into the forest, but they had no clue what fruit it was. She mentioned that the Sasquatch showed her in a vision a small watermelon-looking fruit, but the insides were not too sweet, and they were green, and the seeds were black.

Since no one knew what it was, I took off for my hike. The weird thing is that when I reached the summit, I found a vine on the ground, and I followed it, and the very fruit that the Sasquatch described to my friend was attached to the vine, growing wild.

The crazy thing is that my Native American friend has never traveled outside of the US, and she was able to describe a Spanish fruit that not even the locals knew about.

I was actually glad I didn't have to carry it all the way from the store. I broke it and put it on a rock for them as they had requested.

As I was hiking down, I noticed the typical pushed-over trees which were near the trail. However, these were extremely strong eucalyptus trees, and they had been clearly pushed over the hiking trail, and there were also footprints there.

I found, not too far from there, a huge ancient Spanish wall that was torn down at a spot where a trampled-down game trail connected. This wall looked like it had been there for hundreds of years, but the damage was fairly recent, as there was no moss on the torn-down rocks that once formed the wall.

The spot was remote, and there would be no human reason to damage it at that specific spot. The force necessary to take down that wall would have required machinery or a very determined, strong person.

All the fallen rocks were on the same outer side of the wall downward from the side of the trail, which looked like whoever knocked it was traveling downhill from the left where the game trail came and intersected the hiking trail and literally plowed down the wall and made its way downhill past it. It was clear that the game trail continued on the other side of the wall.

Maybe the Sasquatch got tired of having to jump the wall and made a hole in it so they could step over it…… it's the only creature that would have enough strength to take down the wall without chipping the rocks into pieces like machinery would, and there were no tracks of vehicles on that trail that would really make sense. I also took videos and pictures as well analyzing how that very thick ancient wall could have been demolished at that remote spot.

From Ferrol, I traveled to the ancient city of Salamanca, Spain, where the world-renowned university of Salamanca is located and where the original Vaquero (Cowboy) culture came from to America before it was appropriated by the Anglo-Saxons who now want to claim it as their own by erasing Spanish history but cowboys are Spanish in origin.

Then I traveled to Merida, Spain, where the ancient Roman ruins and aqueducts are located, and spent some marvelous days exploring and enjoying the good weather and food.

By now, it was about to be Christmas, and I really wasn't feeling like staying in Spain during Christmas as I needed rest. Spain is very festive during that season, so I headed back to Sintra, Portugal, and got a bed in a coastal town near Sintracalled Collares, which was the perfect choice because the Portuguése stay home during Christmas, and I pretty much had the whole hostel to myself with awesome views, near the beach and I had nothing but peace and quiet.

During this time, I met a girl from China at the hostel. She was taking surfing lessons nearby, and she was a science major and was studying quantum physics; she had a theory that quantum physics was closely linked to the spiritual realm.

So, another very special spiritual connection occurred, and we went to the Quinta De Regaliera castle; I was able to Spiritually activate her there, and it happened right above the caves where the sigil of Lucifer was located.

I did some more grid work during our visit, and It's amazing how easy it was to invert those negative portals and reclaim those structures for the light!!

Thus far, I have rented an electric mountain bike, explored a large area of the Sintra forest and found some massive Sasquatch structures in other areas of the forest near Cascais.

Finally, Christmas came, and I had a beautiful encounter with God while sitting alone on Christmas night by the nearby cliffs overlooking the dark ocean. It was just me and Spirit, and by now, I was becoming proficient at remaining in a mindset of gratitude.

CHAPTER EIGHTEEN
Porto, Amsterdam and Munich

After Christmas, I felt relaxed and renewed. I'm glad I had listened to my body and rested. I made sure I was taking multivitamins constantly and ate as healthy as possible.

It was time to head to Porto, Portugal, to finally catch my plane to Amsterdam. I did an amazing bike route on the north side of the Douro River, along the coast of Porto, and Spirit kept pushing me further north up the coast. I stopped to get a coffee and a croissant at a beach establishment, and the local vibe was really comfortable.

Finally, I ended up at a beach where there was a lot of surfing, and I stopped by a wall that was above the beach. There was a young man playing the drums, and I really felt like I needed to play along with my flute.

I eventually felt the pull so strong to get the guy's attention from above, and he motioned to go down and meet him.

As we introduced ourselves, we struck up a deep conversation about spirituality and, of course, about the Sasquatch as well, and we ended up opening a portal together at the beach just in time for the sunset.

It was another divine appointment with channeled messages for him and a spiritual activation, and I know I will meet him again as I feel there is purpose since he does shamanic and healing work and events and sells real estate. What are the chances of meeting spiritual people and having deep connections and spiritual conversations over and over in Europe?

It seemed that I was not only being led to structures but to people who needed an activation or a spiritual download or something, and I always had something to receive from them as well.

Europe seemed to me like a very magical place during this trip. Actually, I scored 100% average at finding Sasquatch structures every time I went to the forest and people to activate every time I had a conversation.

Now, the time came to leave for Amsterdam, and I had the energy to face the party scene and the chaos of New Year celebrations.

I was fortunate to realize that there was a bicycle shop right in front of my hostel. The weather was cold, wet, and dingy most of the time with permanent inversion, but the people were quite warm and friendly.

I could have visited something else, but I ended up having a great time and assisting in a free concert that was attended by eighty thousand people. I perfected the crowd-biking skills that I learned at the beach boardwalks and eventually headed to Munich, Germany, which was also quite an adventure.

I found the people in Munich and Amsterdam quite familiar compared to the US but, of course, with many different aspects of culture and education.

230630

CHAPTER NINETEEN
Sasquatch in Austria and Slovakia

Finally, I arrived in Vienna. My friend Joseph and I met downtown, and it was awesome seeing him after years of weekly sword practice. He was working as an English tutor and had an apartment lease with several roommates.

I had been sharing about my experiences during my trip about the Sasquatch, and one of his roommates wanted to go to the forest with me. I was again amazed at how quickly we were led to the Sasquatch structures, and by this time, it was quite repetitive. We took videos and pictures of structures and footprints, and I stayed there for quite a few days.

I found that Vienna is a beautiful city and way too convenient, and it was hard to leave. At the same time, I found the Austrians to be not as friendly as in the Netherlands, but we managed to have a good time visiting many different landmarks and eating out. I made another trip to the forest, and every time I was there, I found more and more structures.

It was hard to believe that there would be so many Sasquatch structures in Austria, but I realized that they live everywhere where there is forest and they act as protectors of nature and in Europe, people don't go camping as much, and they don't carry guns like they do in the US so the forests are more intact and the Sasquatch go mostly unnoticed so their population could potentially be much higher than in the US the further you go east in Europe.

On one occasion, Joseph wanted to go on a bike ride with me, and we rented bikes and traveled along the Danube River to the outskirts of town until he had to turn around to go to work.

I continued and realized that there was a natural reserve right next to us and decided to bike there and take a look. I again found some massive structures and a giant hunting trap made by the Sasquatch, very similar to the one I found in Oregon while I was exploring with my Native American friend.

The hunting trap was next to a trail and started out wide, but it narrowed into these massive entrances made of trees that were carefully placed upside down and had no root system attached to them.

The tree trunks had been brought there and placed, forming a gate about 8 feet tall, and it was made of different types of trees that had been lifted and placed masterfully.

Then, the pathway funneled into a carefully designed labyrinth made of trees that were arranged in such a way that once an animal entered and walked deep enough into the twisty labyrinth, if it got spooked and tried to escape, it would run into everything, but the exit and it would be easy to harvest it at that point.

As I was describing it while shooting the video and explaining how the structure had been built, the video captured an audible hoot from a Sasquatch in the distance.

Finally, my friend Joseph gave me different suggestions of places to visit before leaving Vienna, and I headed for Bratislava, Slovakia, in the Balkans.

It was interesting to be in a town that once was under strict communism, but it now was lovely, and the women were very attractive. After visiting the town and exploring the cafes and restaurants for a couple of days, I asked the front desk clerk to give me some suggestions for hiking.

Outside of the charming city, there was a ski area that had not gotten any snow for the season yet. Now, I was noticing a pattern because I met on the bus another girl who was very interested in the Sasquatch research I was doing; she worked at the tourist area where I was heading and accompanied me and led me straight to the hiking trails.

As we were walking, I mentioned the smaller type of structures that I had found in Portugal and Austria, and she mentioned that they had them all over the area in that forest as well and that they saw them all the time but didn't know who built them.

Later, I had a realization that in order to open portals properly, there had to be male and female energy present, and every time I found structures and opened portals, a local female was with me.

I only met one male who was the guy at the beach in Portugal, but there were no structures, and the rest were females, but he was a spiritual leader type, and I'm sure he was going to spiritually activate females later.

CHAPTER TWENTY
The Bosnian Pyramids

It had been 2 months since I had arrived in Europe, where I traveled from country to country, and going into Bosnia was an interesting experience full of intense moments.

On the bus from Zagreb, Croatia, to Visoko, Bosnia, where the pyramids are located, we got stopped at a passport checkpoint, and all the passengers had to exit the bus to get questioned by the authorities. They were checking me out hard and longer than anyone else.

After some questioning and passport verifications, we began the trip again, only to be stopped a few minutes ahead again, and they collected all of our passports. Eventually, they gave them back, but by now, people were stressed out.

I was sitting in the very back with a group of students from Spain, and they all thought I was trouble of some kind and were talking about me, saying that I was probably a gipsy or a terrorist without realizing that I understood everything they were saying.

It was the middle of the night, to begin with, and when we finally got back on the bus, I put on my sunglasses the dark bus and my kaya (Muslim men's scarf) over my head and kept staring at them quietly and very serious from the back of the bus for the rest of the trip, and that totally freaked them out. That was fun messing with their already stressed-out and sheltered young minds.

Cold, windy road, it felt like we were entering the twilight zone. I'm surprised no one vomited from all the sharp turns on a 2-lane road full of roundabouts going super-fast in the middle of snowy and pitch dark nowhere in Bosnia. It was the red-eye bus ride from hell.

All of a sudden, everyone got a message from their phone providers saying we had no more gigabytes left, so no one had cellphone access. About a week after this phase of my Euro trip, I was talking to a girl in Slovenia, which is right next to Bosnia, and I found out that when you leave the European Union, they steal all your data as you cross into Bosnia.

My check-in time at my apartment was not until noon, and I got dropped off at 4:15 am in the middle of this dark 1 gas station in the rural town of Visoko, Bosnia, in 26-degree weather.

I put on my ski pants, beanie, and all the layers I had. I had had enough sense to bring a very packable sleeping bag and a hammock, and I set it up between the only 2 poles close enough to each other in the whole town that could hold my hammock, which was conveniently located 7 steps from where I got dropped off.

I got in my sleeping bag and onto the hammock and slept for a few hours warm and cozy with my backpack on top of me.

I was awakened by Muslim chants coming from a speaker above my head and from local passersby as they were heading to work really early as the new day got rolling. Eventually, I got up to ask a passerby where to get a SIM card, and he pointed me to a stand literally steps away from my hammock.

What are the chances!! Perfect spot to be dropped off in the middle of the night. I really had to trust that I'd be taken care of, and it didn't disappoint at all.

I then looked on my maps and looked up, I realized that I was right next to the pyramid of the Sun and a 5-minute walk from my apartment.

I waited at a coffee shop, where I also realized that the national sport of choice in Bosnia is smoking indoors. I came out of the café smelling like a cigar. Finally, I got a hold of the apartment owner, and he allowed me to check in early, although he was strangely rude and asked me if I was from a cartel.

The apartment was amazing with 2 balconies, modern, 2 bedrooms, kitchen, large bathroom with hot tub and next to the river with a view of the pyramid and the best part was that it cost me €45 for 3 nights.

After settling, I went to take a walk and buy some groceries, and I noticed that people were all staring at me hard and mumbling. I didn't know if I was doing anything wrong. It was very persistent, and after shopping, going out to eat, and walking around, I went back to the apartment and looked up the history of the area.

I found out there was a massive genocide and ethnic cleansing war in which millions of Muslims, gipsies, and other ethnic groups were brutally murdered, the headcount was astronomical, and the UN had to intervene.

Now the vibe I got made sense; so much trauma in the air. The ethnic cleansing event was recent enough as it took place in the 80s to where almost all of the mature people there would have been involved, and many felt to me like they could have been war criminals.

I had to really tap in spiritually to transmute the local energy around me and what I was noticing. This was a spiritual boot camp that I hadn't experienced yet. I realized that I had to remain in a state of gratitude to be able to deal with the darkness of the place.

I also noticed that through the land, there are more graveyards than anywhere in the world I've ever seen, and I picked up on the darkness that lingered under the surface.

I was still amazed to be at this prime spot that Spirit set me up in. It had a view of the pyramid of the Sun from my room and balcony. It was a super nice apartment, and the price was unbeatable. I knew it was divinely meant to be till I finished the spiritual work I was there to do.

I did some grid work by the river in my front yard under the pyramid and relaxed for the first day. I knew it was going to get interesting the next day.

My tour lady picked me up at 11. The price was steep for a 2-day tour, but I felt I needed to go forward with it. I shared about my Sasquatch research with the lady as we were heading to the different archeological sites, and she happened to be really open to my stories and spiritual perspectives, and we established a really good rapport.

The excavations were not so visually impressive, but the energy was off the charts.

We came up to a mount, of course, next to a bunch of graveyards, and Spirit wanted me to start playing the flute in a hurry, so I asked for permission from my guide to play at the center of the ceremonial stone circle at the top of the mount, and as I started playing, the high vibration went off the charts, and then I started channeling light language super loud.

Needless to say, this was extremely impactful for my guide as she stood in the distance listening. She got blasted with the energy of the Spirit that was released, and it was no small thing.

She later took me to the pyramid of the moon and later to the trails at the pyramid of the Sun. There, we found freshly broken trees that were clear markings of the Sasquatch, and she mentioned that she had been there 3 days prior, and the trees were not broken, and they were in an area that was extremely difficult for humans to reach and they were both broken, pointing in the same direction but about 20 feet apart from each other and the breaks on the trees were too high for a human to reach.

We also found some glyphs written on the ground with sticks, which were very similar to the recorded glyphs that my Native American friend's son recorded at their property in northern Idaho and also similar to the glyphs engraved on a rock inside the tunnels of the Pyramid of the Sun however no one knew what the glyphs meant.

When we compared the glyphs from Idaho, the glyphs from the sticks we found on the ground, and the glyphs from the Bosnian pyramids, they were eerily similar.

We also found the iconic leaning stick that the Sasquatch left to allow people to communicate with them telepathically, so she kept it. We both knew the Sasquatch were there. We both could feel them as well.

Later, she took me to the tunnels, and the energy there was astoundingly positive. Apparently, the pyramid has the ability to invert negative energy, and Bosnia really needed it. The tunnels had many meditation chambers, and people have reported receiving healing by meditating in those tunnels.

The temperature was very pleasant, with lots of humidity, and the tunnel system had no end. At the end of the day, we had more questions than answers, and I was led to play and pray to cleanse the energy of the area at many spots.

On the second day, we headed to climb the pyramid of the Sun. The fog was extremely thick, the road was icy, and my guide waited in her car while I climbed the pyramid as the trails were too muddy and slippery for her to climb.

Not strangely, I had the whole pyramid to myself. I reached the top and immediately was led to play and release light language and prayers to amplify the divine Spirit consciousness, Holy Spirit or however you want to call it, over the earth as the lay lines there are numerous, and the pyramid amplifies and transports the energy.

This occurred not surprisingly at 11:33 am Bosnia time on the US Inauguration Day.

What are the chances of this happening without planning it!

I have time and GPS-stamped pictures of everything I'm mentioning as well.

The prayers that I was led to release in light language were extremely intense, and when I played the flute, all the nearby animals started going crazy, making lots of noise, and my guide could hear me playing all the way from where she was parked.

Later, my guide took me back to the tunnels and showed me the museum and the park. Some of the stones found in the pyramid were like from a sci-fi movie.

We toured the many ceremonial and meditation structures at their park, and when we got to the sculptures of the fairies, she began to tell me about the many local and cultural legends they have about them.

I shared how I actually swatted a fairy that flew by my face at a didgeridoo festival in Oregon as my friend David watched the whole thing unfold, and as soon as I said that to my tour guide, a small pebble hit the thin metal pole that was next to us very loudly and startled us.

We looked around, and there was not a soul nearby. We continued talking about the local legends of the fairies, and another small rock hit the thin metal pole. We realized that it was either the Sasquatch or the fairies throwing rocks at us, but there were no people anywhere in sight.

They definitely had to have good aim to hit the thin metal pole so well and twice. This actually seemed to startle my guide, so we walked away and continued with the tour to check out the different structures, medicine wheels, meditation spirals, labyrinths, and sculptures as she was telling me how, during the high season, there are many spiritual gatherings, concerts and metaphysical events.

Eventually, my guide needed to go to the bathroom, which was situated at the end of the property by the creek, and I decided I needed to go as well. When I got close to the bathroom, I noticed that there were Sasquatch structures right next to the creek past the bathrooms at their property.

I mentioned it to her, and we went into the woods to check them out. I took videos and pictures as well. I never expected to find structures right there at the base of the pyramid, but it made sense that they would be there, and it all seemed divinely orchestrated.

I gave her many instructions as to how to communicate with the Sasquatch, and I think it's going to get really interesting for her as the Sasquatch showed up a lot during our tour. I hope to hear back from her about what happens next.

Finally, the checkout day came. I really felt I needed to make my way out of Bosnia and into Split, Croatia, and my bus to Croatia was booked for 3 pm, leaving from Sarajevo.

I had been told that it was better to take the train from Visoko to Sarajevo. Checkout time came, and very conveniently and rudely, the owner of the apartment came to kick me out at 10:30 am, demanding 5-star reviews. I was already packed, and something had told me to leave the place spotless, and I'm glad I did.

After the awkward moment, I headed to the train station on foot to catch the train to Sarajevo, which was scheduled to depart from Visoko at 11:30

am, only to find out that the route was closed for the winter. I had to get to Sarajevo before 3 to catch my bus. As I was making my way back to town, a bus that said Sarajevo passed by.

I was about to get a cab that would have cost me €30 to get there, but I asked some girls where I could catch a bus to Sarajevo, and the station was just around the corner. As I pulled up to the bus station, immediately the bus came, and I was on my way.

I had time to check out downtown Sarajevo and get a coffee. Sarajevo is a major city, and it had a slightly better vibe than Visoko. I noticed there were many mosques throughout the land, and many were surrounded by graveyards that probably belonged to the Muslims who were killed in the war. It was a mix of Eastern block culture with Middle Eastern culture.

Even at the downtown park, there were mass graveyards, and I was led to open portals by playing my flute and praying in light language so the souls could leave and finally rest.

I got on the bus, and 2 hours later, we got stuck in the mountains for another 2 hours as there had been a massive accident just ahead of our bus on the treacherous 2-lane road, we then went through another grueling border checkpoint and finally, I made out of Bosnia and into Split, Slovenia which is a really cool beach city and I was able to relax right away.

What a nice town with beautiful views, a daily farmer's market, and tons of outdoor things to do. Actually, it was an awesome experience going to Bosnia, but I know the energies there didn't want to be messed with, and that's what I was sent there to do.

What are the chances that I was at the top of the pyramid doing grid work to bring down the powers that shouldn't be at 11:33 am on Inauguration Day? I didn't plan it that way. I also don't pay attention nor take sides in politics, and my prayers are in Light Language as I don't need to know any unnecessary details. I wasn't surprised that I had the whole pyramid to myself, as the heavy fog kept people from wanting to go there.

While I was in Split, I rented a bicycle to check out the city, and I ended up in the mountains. I was led to open a portal at the top next to the viewpoint near a cross that overlooked the bay, and as I was coming down the forest on a trail, Spirit told me to stop and to walk to my left, and I found a Sasquatch structure with a leaned tree and 3 quartz rocks forming a triangle at the base of the tree with a quartz rock in the center. What are the chances!!

I took videos and pictures, played my flute, opened a portal, headed downhill, and found a perfect spot with a viewpoint and a coffee shop. I ordered a coffee and a chocolate croissant end and relaxed, admiring the gorgeous views of the Balkan sea.

RUNIC SYMBOLS
RUNSKO PISMO

Wednesday 22 January
11:33

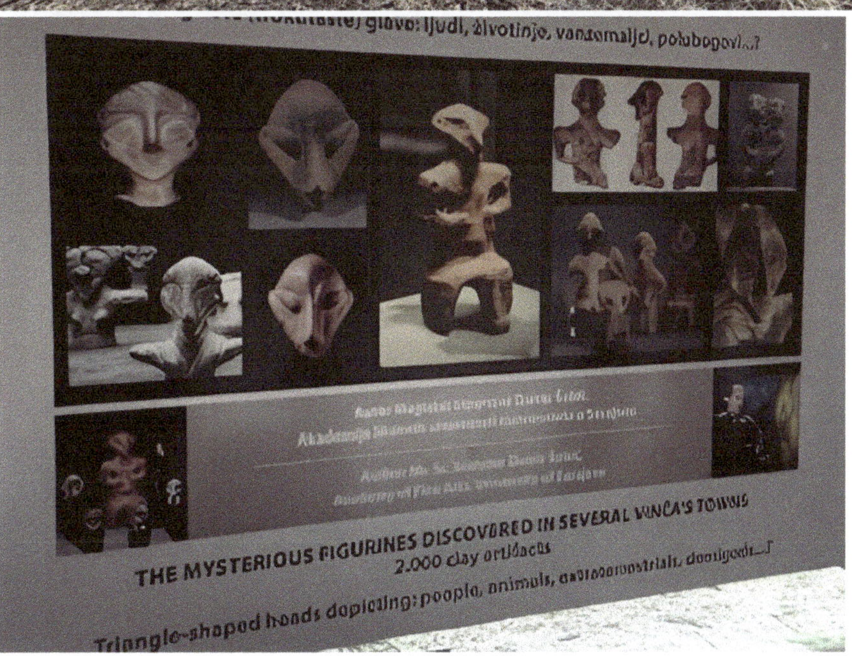
...... (trokutaste) glave: ljudi, životinje, vanzemaljci, polubogovi...?
THE MYSTERIOUS FIGURINES DISCOVERED IN SEVERAL VINCA'S TOWNS
2.000 clay artifacts
Triangle-shaped heads depicting: people, animals, extraterrestrials, demigods...?

Horizontal Syllabic Patterns

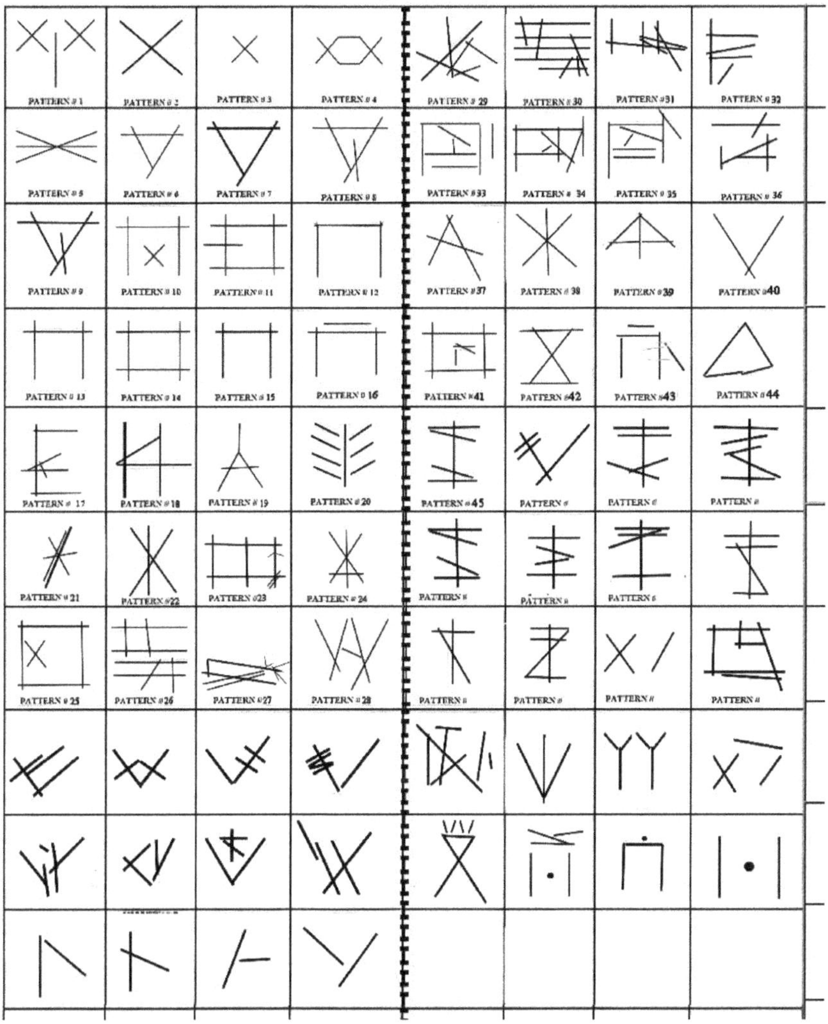

PATTERN # 1	PATTERN # 2	PATTERN # 3	PATTERN # 4	PATTERN # 29	PATTERN # 30	PATTERN # 31	PATTERN # 32
PATTERN # 5	PATTERN # 6	PATTERN # 7	PATTERN # 8	PATTERN # 33	PATTERN # 34	PATTERN # 35	PATTERN # 36
PATTERN # 9	PATTERN # 10	PATTERN # 11	PATTERN # 12	PATTERN # 37	PATTERN # 38	PATTERN # 39	PATTERN # 40
PATTERN # 13	PATTERN # 14	PATTERN # 15	PATTERN # 16	PATTERN # 41	PATTERN # 42	PATTERN # 43	PATTERN # 44
PATTERN # 17	PATTERN # 18	PATTERN # 19	PATTERN # 20	PATTERN # 45	PATTERN #	PATTERN #	PATTERN #
PATTERN # 21	PATTERN # 22	PATTERN # 23	PATTERN # 24	PATTERN #	PATTERN #	PATTERN #	PATTERN #
PATTERN # 25	PATTERN # 26	PATTERN # 27	PATTERN # 28	PATTERN #	PATTERN #	PATTERN #	PATTERN #

CHAPTER TWENTY-ONE
The Giant Caves in Italy

My time in Split, Croatia, came all too quickly, and I headed toward Italy. I arrived at the coast of Trieste, Italy, which borders Slovenia. I actually liked the cultural vibe of Italy quite a bit.

The city sits on the coast of the Adriatic Sea in the Gulf of Trieste, of course. It is a quaint town, and I was able to understand a lot of Italian; it became easy for me to speak what I knew. I explored the fortresses and city, but the highlight came later.

When I was in Split, Croatia, I was talking to the hostel clerk girl, and she mentioned the giant caves in Slovenia, a 30-minute drive from Trieste. I was planning to go visit, but it was difficult without a car, so I talked to the front desk at the Trieste hostel, and the girl told me that Trieste also had a giant cave system that connected to the one in Slovenia, but it was in the outskirts of Trieste, and buses ran there often.

I found some caves that were listed as free entrance or open 24/7 and took the bus to the area, I found them, but they were for professionals with gear and equipment to rappel into them, and the entrance was very dangerous and more like a hole in the ground that went straight down, but it was nice to walk around the forest again and get some fresh air.

The cave system that the girl at the desk had told me about was closed on Sunday, and I made the decision to book another night at the hostel to go see them the next day. I called early to book my cave tour, and I realized it was raining very hard, but I found a break where it stopped raining for a short time to go catch the bus and buy some food on the way.

As the bus was approaching, the rain turned into a monsoon, and I got off the bus along with a family and their 2 kids from Russia; we all took shelter under a bus stop while the rain got way out of control.

The thunder was insane as we all stood like sardines under the roof of the tiny bus stop.

It was forming a river on the street, but we managed to stay dry. I put on my umbrella hat, which allowed me to use my hands freely, and started eating while I waited for the rain to diminish.

I was proud of myself for packing exactly what I was going to need and nothing else.

The family took off in the rain towards the cave as we were all going to take the same tour, and I arrived later after I finished my food. We were the only tourists on the whole tour, and we were assigned a really friendly Italian girl as a guide.

The caves were incredibly deep, there were five thousand steps to reach the bottom, and the views were absolutely breathtaking.

The guide girl mentioned that I was lucky enough to come on a very rainy day, so there were only a few people in the cave.

Normally, the groups can be as big as 120 people. The guide told me that it is extremely rare to have rain where you could see the multiple waterfalls come alive in the cave, and she was excited to let me play my flute inside.

The sound and the experience were amazing, and she shot a video of my performance. Everyone seemed to like the sound, and it was an unforgettable experience.

She mentioned that during the summer, they have concerts because the acoustics are so good.

It had been definitely worth it booking the extra day in Trieste to see this beauty of a place which is in the Guinness World Record for the largest cave system in Europe.

The tour was absolutely fantastic, and I was able to play as well in a tunnel system as we were ascending from the main cave. Obviously, I opened a portal there as well. She then asked me, when we were almost at the top, ready to exit, if I could play my flute for the tour down below behind us to hear. I was super happy to be given the opportunity to do it, and the sound and the echo were just phenomenal.

My flute has an engraved symbol of a trinity, and the girl happened to have a tattoo on her leg of the same symbol. Again, another cool synchronicity. I spent the rest of the day visiting the city, and finally, I took a red-eye bus to Rome with a scale in Bologna, and the trip was something to remember.

There was no other way to get to Rome from where I was, and the buses so far had been very comfortable. The bus was full of Bosnians, Hindus, Italians, Germans, and who knows what else, and it was unusually packed for a red-eye schedule.

This trip to Europe has opened my eyes to the complexities of global immigration and travel. And by now, I had figured out that gratitude was the best antidote for having a bad attitude.

I had to ask a guy from India to move out of my assigned seat. This caused a pretty hilarious effect as he didn't have a seat assigned and tried to sit next to a Bosnian who didn't want him there.

Hearing them argue in really bad English was hilarious to begin with. The guy next to me was from India as well, and he was leaning on my shoulder as he slept hard. he smelled like curry mixed with sweat.

Later, he started snoring in my ear, and I kept pushing him and elbowing him, and he wouldn't stop. I thought to myself, "This is the deepest sleeper by far I've ever seen. The kicks, elbowing, and shoving don't wake him up".

Finally, he woke up, and I tried to tell him he was snoring in my ear, but he seemed puzzled, so I snored one time loudly in his ear as he didn't seem to understand my English, and with a smile, he pointed at the guy, behind us.

About an hour later, I realized what was happening, and I looked at him and apologized out loud because I didn't know the guy snoring was in the seat behind him. He was pretty patient as I elbowed him through the night, and when I apologized, the German couple, who had been watching the whole thing unfold in amazement, locked eyes with me as I turned, and we all started laughing out loud. Everyone else started laughing.

We all had a good laugh, of course, except for the Bosnians; they just didn't laugh, and the one snoring was Bosnian.

Later, at the next stop, we watched an onboarding passenger kick another Indian guy out of his seat, and we all giggled as it was happening all over again.

Then, the German guy really needed to go to the bathroom, and he couldn't figure out how to open the door. It was one of those moments when you couldn't stop laughing if you tried.

Kudos to the poor guy I kept hitting. He was being such a good sport. The essence of the book was working, and I was able to see the humor in what could have been a stressful situation.

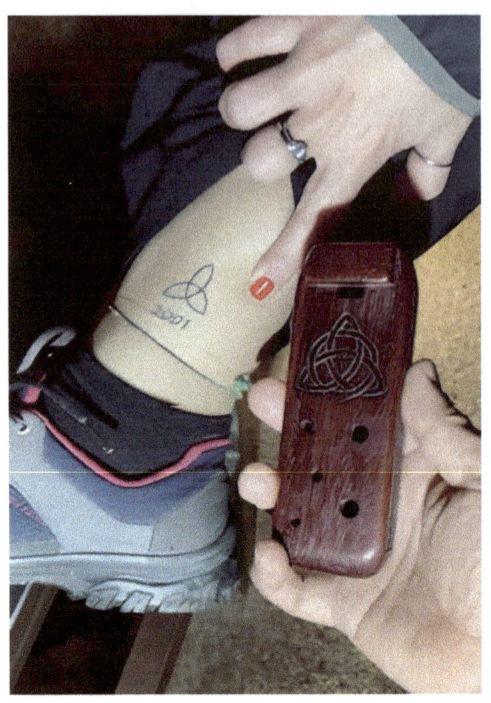

CHAPTER TWENTY-TWO
Sasquatch in Rome? You Bet!

Rome is one of those places worth visiting more than once.

It's like Barcelona; there is always something new to see. By now, I was really getting to like the Italian culture.

I think my 3 favorite or most compatible cultures in Europe would have to be Italy, Portugal, and Croatia. But for sure, in Italy, although it was slightly more expensive than Portugal and Croatia and the food portions were pretty much a ripoff in most cases, the vibe, for a capital, was very comfortable, polite, and accepting, although it was overridden by tourism all year round.

I did my regular tour of the main sites of Rome, including the Coliseum, the fountain of Trevi, and so on, for the first couple of days, and at some point, I knew I was supposed to go to the Vatican to invert the portals that the pope had recently opened.

The way Spirit presented it to me was that it takes a tremendous amount of dark rituals and energy to make a negative portal even work, but someone who is aligned with God spiritually can open portals really easily, and they are permanent because the main energy of the universe is positive energy, and by now, I had opened enough portals in sketchy places that the Vatican didn't seem like anything different.

As I was heading on the bus to the Vatican, S the bus passed by a fountain that I had not seen at the top of a hill near a park, and I got off to take a look. I took a few pictures and went to the bus stop, only to miss the next bus.

I looked on Google Maps and saw that there was a park nearby on the way to the Vatican and that there was a whole area with a fountain that worshipped the image of the Satyr or the devil, and it was eerily similar to the sculptures in Sintra with devils and goats carved on a giant cup.

As I entered the park through an arch, I was shown to open a portal at the summit, and as I was going to play my flute to open the portal, a girl sat nearby, and I was shown to play while she was there because the portal needed male and female energy.

Once I was done, I started heading towards the fountain of the Satyr, and as I was following the trail, I was pulled strongly towards a smaller tail that led to a fence behind the bushes.

When I got there, to my amazement, behind the fence was a Sasquatch structure with a large X made of two trees upside down and a giant asterisk made of several trees that had been

placed, and there were several trees that were bent over the fence. As I examined the structures, I came to the conclusion that the structure was built long after the fence was built because no one would have built that fence without first removing or cutting the trees that were bent and leaning over it from the inside towards the outside of the fence.

I also noticed that the structure and the park sat well above the altitude of the Vatican, and the Sasquatch showed me that they had built the structures to open a portal to counteract the portals that the Vatican had opened recently and that they wanted humans who were aligned spiritually with the light to open portals where they had made structures to make them stronger.

They also showed me that the powers that shouldn't be are required to show people exactly what they are doing before they do it and that if no one says anything, they are in silent agreement with what the dark powers are trying to make us manifest for them.

They showed me that what we have to do is disagree with what they are doing, raise a complaint to the heavenly realm, and assign and deploy the spiritual forces, who are supposed to carry out the changes that need to happen on earth, to undo the works of darkness, and that we don't need to do anything else. That's the job of the angelic and of the spiritual alliances of the Light.

So, instead of keeping our mouths shut and letting them do what they want, we need to get busy following those instructions, and the Sasquatch are our allies.

After that, I headed to the Vatican, and what are the chances that when I got to the frontcourt by the obelisk and was told by Spirit to start opening portals by playing my flute and using light language, it was 3:33 pm Rome time. No one can make that up; not only that, but there was a moment when the clouds opened momentarily, and the sun hit me in the face before the clouds closed down again, and this is not a joke. I felt it was some sign of divine confirmation for me.

By the time I had finished doing my prayer rounds inside the Vatican and came out to the front court, it was 4:55 pm. Now, as Jesus said, it is finished!

The following day, I went to the Roman catacombs. A reservation was not required, but they had specific times when they gave tours in different languages. I'm not sure how it happened, but I arrived exactly 5 minutes before the last tour in English was about to take place.

It was cold outside, but the temperature inside the caves was a permanent 55 degrees Fahrenheit, and the humidity was about 95 percent all year round.

These were the caves where the early Christians were buried as thousands of them were thrown in with the lions at the Coliseums for refusing to worship the Caesars and rebelling against the establishment.

One thing I noticed was that at other graveyard sights, there were very heavy energies that I had to open portals for to let the souls leave and go to rest. At these catacombs, the energy was very peaceful, and I felt pleasant and comfortable.

I didn't feel like I needed to do anything special.

One thing I noticed was that on the wall, the tour guide pointed out a catholic symbol made of an X and a P that together made an asterisk. She mentioned that the X means Christ and the P means Peace, and all of a sudden, I remembered the Sasquatch structure at the park above the Vatican the day before had an X standing alone and an asterisk on the ground. I also remembered that my Native American friend had mentioned to me that she had asked the Sasquatch if they knew who Jesus Christ was, and they responded, "The man that walked on water?" And they told her that they have immense respect for him. Coincidentally, she messaged me and asked me if I had seen the representations of the Sasquatch in the Vatican, which I didn't know anything about and lo and behold, there are representations of the Sasquatch right at the bottom of Michelangelo's painting in the Sistine Chapel right where the cross is, over the depiction of what they called, the underworld part of the painting and anyone can look them up online or see them in person.

Later on, when I arrived in Sevilla and was eating Sushi with my friend from Iran, we noticed that the symbol of the restaurant was an X, and I had just shared about the asterisk and the cave story with her an hour prior.

The X at Sasquatch structures is extremely common. My Native American friend told me that it also represents exchange, so you are supposed to bring an offering to them when you enter their territory as a sign of respect for the work they do to protect the forest and to ask for permission to be in the forest as everything in nature must be treated with the utmost respect.

My editor, while reviewing my book, later sent me videos of a Native American chief that explained the Hopi prophecies, and she mentioned that there were 2 groups of humans, the white-skinned humans who originated towards the east of the American continent would be drawn to materialism, wars, and technology that eventually would destroy themselves and the earth and the brown-skinned people who were in charge of preserving the spiritual connection and the well-being of the earth. I also watched a documentary where someone pointed out that the large medallion that Queen Elizabeth wore depicts a white fallen angel who is stepping over the head of a colored man, and he explained that the colored man had the seed of Adam. Coincidentally, people of all colors and nations are waking up spiritually to see and change what's going on.

She sent me the Hopi prophecies video after I had shared a video of an ex 3 letter agency agent who used to be a real "man in black" who was trained to kill people who were exposing things, and he mentioned that the government had made alliances with alien beings, in exchange for technology to reduce the human population from 6 billion to 800 million through poisoning the waters, food supply, the so-called health care system and wars and famines and that, unfortunately is a reality today.

That very message was engraved on the Georgia Guidestones, which later got bombed and destroyed. Coincidentally, during the writing of my book, I had read the book of Daniel in the Bible about the king's dream of the statue, which represents the kingdoms and systems of the world, and both the Hopi prophecies and the book of Daniel describe the same events. Including the Hopi parallel with what Christians would call the return of Christ, the destruction of those who would follow the path of materialism, the preservation of the survivors who did not follow materialism and government control, and the establishment of his never-ending kingdom.

My take is that we are now living in the days of the fulfillment of those prophecies.

Thursday 30 January
3:33

CHAPTER TWENTY-THREE
The 7 Headed Dragons

As I was showering and pondering about this book I'm writing, I realized that this book is no different than how the apostles lived and wrote their experiences, which later were deified by some cult to control the minds of people.

I didn't write any pertinent names to keep my friends' participation in my life story from being misused. A gospel is an account of events that happened in someone's life, and that's it. We all have a gospel inside of us. Even my friend, who drives like a bat out of hell in the US, has one.

Also, I must say that we need as humans to start listening to our own hearts because we possess the divine universal knowledge to guide us through life, and we have been conditioned to be so lazy that we depend on others to tell us what to do.

This reminds me of the meme of the Dragon in the Clouds that is telling a chicken: "Remember who you are," and the chicken is just sitting there with a bubble over its head filled with question marks.

Not surprisingly, I came across on Instagram a video of the 7 headed dragons or wisdom bringers known as the Nagas in India, which are also found in Siberia and in Native American culture, they embody the 7 systems or chakras in the body and allow you to liberate yourself from over-identification with the temporary existence of the body and embrace the reality that we are eternal beings.

What struck me is that there is a depiction of King Arthur fighting the 7 headed dragon, which to me represents the powers that shouldn't be, fighting to make humans forget our divine wisdom so they can control the world.

Shortly after the catacomb visit, I got a cold, but I had already seen Rome, and I had done what I was supposed to do, and I had enough days booked at my hostel to get over it, rest and head to Sevilla, where I was going to catch the plane to fly back home.

During the time that I was sick, I had a vivid dream of me fighting with my mother, and as I was getting more and more mad at her, I came to a point in my dream where I stopped, and I started crying and apologized to her and forgave her.

I feel that this was the divine revelation of the root cause of my rage in my childhood and that the Spirit gave me the breakthrough in a dream, and I felt so much better afterward.

My opinion about this is that whatever changes or healing Spirit leads us to make or experience in our lives to improve our current behavioral patterns, the Spirit will also give us supernatural assistance to bring us the necessary breakthrough in our ascension process, and we are not alone in healing ourselves.

CHAPTER TWENTY-FOUR
Chico De Gallo — New Beginnings

It was a beautiful afternoon out on the hiking trail. I had decided to go on a spiritual walk as I had been feeling depleted and lost recently.

My wife had been in the hospital with a serious condition, and she had barely made it alive. She had just been released from the hospital.

It was one of those days when I really needed to reconnect with Spirit. As I walked down the trail, I noticed a strange bird that kept following me. It almost looked like a hawk, but it wasn't injured, and it wasn't flying. It just kept walking behind me at a distance. During my walk, I experienced a special and powerful moment with God in which I felt a strong reconnection, and eventually, I started heading back to my car only to realize that the bird was still following me.

As I arrived at the parking lot, a friend pulled up on his truck to say hi to me while I was getting ready to leave. We had a good conversation, and we both were amazed as we noticed that the bird was walking around my ankles in circles. We had a good laugh about it, and he took off, leaving me alone in the parking lot with this strange bird as the sun was setting.

I had no idea what was happening, but the bird let me pick it up, and I jokingly started asking him questions to find out what he wanted, who he was, and if he needed anything.

It was the strangest thing to be talking to this bird, so I had to take some selfies with it sitting on my arm. It seemed extremely comfortable with me and almost seemed like it was posing for the camera.

I finally put it down and told it that it was time to go home. As I put it on the ground, the bird looked at my car and approached the open door while looking back at me. I said out loud, "You are not thinking of jumping in my car, are you?"

The bird looked at me, looked at the stepping rail, and jumped into my car while I took pictures and proceeded to sit on the passenger seat and waited there, looking at me with an expression of almost saying, "Are we leaving or what??"

I thought to myself, "This is the weirdest day ever," so I took him home and brought him to my wife's bed as she was recovering, and the bird went right up next to her and started cuddling by her face as if it was trying to comfort her.

My wife eventually recovered, and the months following were absolutely amazing as this bird adjusted immediately to my wife's cats and dogs; it ate at the table with us and wiped its beak on a napkin when it was done eating. It wore a red diaper around the house. We would take him on walks in a stroller, and we were just amazed at how well he got along with everyone.

I would go on drives around town, and the bird would sit on my shoulder, enjoying the ride. I got a lot of attention from people in the cars next to me and even from the police as they looked, pointed, and smiled at us as we were driving along the road.

I would take him on bike rides on a basket. We didn't even know what kind of bird it was since the colors of its feathers were so different, ranging from deep green, brown, red, white, deep blue, black, and yellow, until one day, it started crowing in the backyard. That's when we realized we had a juvenile rooster in our family. It was a rare breed from Chile called Arakana, and the hens lay blue eggs.

I looked up online the meaning of the rooster as a spirit animal, and I kept getting that the message of the rooster was to announce the new dawn and "New Beginnings," we named him "Chico De Gallo," and this little bird brought so much joy to us and everyone around.

The months following were extremely fun, but later, they turned hard as my wife and I were having issues between us as we were facing some hard financial difficulties.

She decided to move to another state to find work, and we ended up divorcing. I remained in the house only to find Chico had passed away one morning. Everything was falling apart.

I tried to reunite with my wife, and we re-married about a year later, only to find that we still had unresolved issues between us, and we ended up marrying and divorcing again and trying to reunite for the third time.

9 years later and just before I embarked on my last trip to Europe, I had a conversation with the Russian energy worker girl that I was dating, and she mentioned to me that she could not be with me because she felt I had unfinished business with my ex-wife, my Iranian friend also mentioned that my ex-wife was the real test to my spiritual growth and that she was my personal "Everest" and that she would not leave my mind until I learned all the lessons.

After returning from the three-month trip that inspired me to write this book, I was in the middle of taking training online to re-enter the workforce, and I noticed that my ex-wife had looked at my profile online.

I had been really worried about her well-being, and I could not get her out of my head during all those years.

At some point, while I was pondering all of this, I remember realizing that the roosters are direct descendants of dinosaurs, which are a form of dragons, and that Chico the rooster had brought a message of joy and self-awareness which was consistent with the messages I had received through my life from the dragons and he came into our lives as a reminder that we are given an opportunity every morning to celebrate life and create a better new beginning.

I was hesitant to contact my ex-wife, so I just sent her a friend request and waited to see what would happen. Shortly after that, she reached out, and eventually, we had a phone call, and she was doing fine. All the issues I was worried about for her had been resolved, and she pointed out that we started talking again ten years later on the very date when we had met for the first time.

During a conversation with my friend from Iran one afternoon, shortly after I started communicating with my ex-wife, she mentioned that the real test in spiritual growth will come to us repeatedly until we learn and integrate all the spiritual lessons that we are supposed to learn in this lifetime.

My friend mentioned to me that there are two different kinds of spirituality. One is based on esoteric outward manifestations like energy healing, miracle work, grid work, and supernatural abilities, and the other involves inner work. It was interesting to realize that the Sasquatch had said the same thing to my native American friend as well and that their message to humanity was to grow spiritually and that we need to raise our internal frequency if we want to survive as a species.

I don't know where things will go from here with my ex-wife or if we should even consider reuniting, but I feel that being self-aware and beginning to apply the lessons learned so far is a good start.

CHAPTER TWENTY-FIVE
My Last Days in Sevilla

When I arrived in Sevilla, I had made plans to meet with my Iranian friend, who I met at the beginning of my trip. We had such a sweet connection, and we were looking forward to meeting each other again.

She had mentioned that she really wanted to spend quality time with me, and I was looking forward to seeing her again. We had some very special moments visiting the ancient baths, eating out, and visiting some nearby towns, and she had some major changes and breakthroughs in her living situation while I was there.

It was definitely an amazing ending to an amazing trip. After a few days, I took my plane to London and my connection to the US. I have to say that I was not tired at all from the trip, and I noticed that I had more sensitivity towards people and energies than I had before.

I went through so many timelines and countries and spiritual densities and cultures and mindsets that I was surprised when I arrived home. I wasn't wiped out, and I recognize that the one thing that preserved my energy was the gratitude I learned to practice during my trip.

Gratitude shifted my energy field and my spiritual disposition to face the mundane challenges and setbacks of traveling, booking stays, and transportation with ease, so much so that I had no resistance in my body and mind, and I was able to let things fall into place.

I'd say that staying in a mindset of gratitude was the most valuable and practical takeaway for me during this trip, and I plan to live my life in a state of gratitude as my cornerstone. And I noticed that if I'm not in a state of gratitude, I'm off spiritually.

I really don't know how this book will impact my readers, but I hope that it makes a difference somehow in someone's life.

The concept of activating people simply means encouraging them to take steps to create a reality beyond their current perceived limitations and to pass on the spiritual juice I have received so they can use it in their walk.

The concept of opening portals is practically esoteric positive energy manipulation placed to flow in a specific region when we receive spiritual guidance to do so. In simple terms, it is blessing the land when and where God says to do it.

The message of the Sasquatch has been an evolving journey, but what I've gathered so far is that we need to get involved consciously, energetically, and spiritually in shifting the global and local realities of the effects of the control that the powers that shouldn't be, are trying to bring upon us and we have to tap into the hidden knowledge and recognize the alliance that the Sasquatch has offered to us to preserve this planet and shift our global reality.

The Sasquatch structures that I found all seem to have different purposes. One that was very obvious was the labyrinth hunting trap, but others are set as portals. It is at these sites where I have done grid work.

The sense I got was that the portal structures counteract the human structures and ancient monuments that have negative energy, and they normally are built inlay lines, and we are a crucial component in reversing the negative portals that other humans or negative beings have set to control the world's energy flow.

I was reminded how, in early 2025, the pope opened 5 portals using black magic in the shape of the Sigil of Lucifer in Rome.

Those portals take an insane amount of dark rituals and tons of planetary alignments to take hold in our realm, and they have to be maintained by more rituals because the universe is made of positive energy, and it's harder for negative energy to remain in portals than positive energy.

I was shown that it only takes one positively spiritually aligned person to open portals of light with no effort, and they are permanent.

Also, I was shown that the dark forces are ritually required to broadcast what they are doing before doing it, and they use the media for that purpose because they do not possess the creative God seed of life, and they are using our consciousness to create or manifest the reality they want while we are sleeping spiritually.

Humans are the ones with the creative power. Not the reptilians who are conjuring pestilences and treatments to reduce the population.

So if we see on TV or in the media that they are doing something awful and we don't protest spiritually, it is like we are giving them permission to use our creative energy to do it.

So, the message that I channeled was clearly that when we see these awful things being done or we see the rituals they are doing on TV right in front of our faces,

or the wars and famines and pestilences they are orchestrating, we have the power and obligation to disagree and place a complaint into the spiritual realm in prayer or meditation, and it's just like calling the cops.

We use our spiritual authority to assign and deploy the angelic and cosmic forces that will be in charge of handling the situation. We complain in prayer and meditation with the intent to disagree and cut the flow of our creative energy that they want to use from us, and we stop what they are showing us by following those specific instructions that I just mentioned, but we are not to get personally involved.

It's the job of the spiritual cops or, in this case, the angels and other allied forces to handle it. The Sasquatch and nature and literally all creation are waiting for humans to step into our place of authority and say enough is enough. The angelic and allied forces cannot be deployed without our command, will, and energy.

We are the demigods here creating our reality with our minds, so it is best to shut the TV off and the social media or watch it as a tool to step into our power and follow those steps now that we know how things work.

The call is to keep this in mind moving forward and start disagreeing by doing the meditations and prayers to handle the horrible things they are trying to do to us, but again, do it without getting personally and energetically involved, if that makes sense.

We need to be completely awake and spiritually activated to do this, or our very human existence is at risk. It's a battle of interplanetary species, Interdimensional hosts of negative energy against humans. We are called to be spiritually activated and ready to face them using our spiritual tools, like the X Men. (Notice the X again)

Just like the movie Star Wars. Reality is weirder than fiction.

The force is with you!! Be activated Now!!

This is not a fiction book but a reality check!

The message of the Dragon, whether it is a real or mythical creature or a spiritual conduit, has been consistent, which is to "Stop being the warrior so we can hold fire for the people," which does not contradict the message of the Sasquatch because it refers to stop being a warrior against mankind and against ourselves.

I realized while I was writing this book that there was a transformative evolution in me during the trip that I took through Europe. I'm not at all saying that my journey is over and I'm a finished product, but there definitely have been some undeniable milestones on my journey and during the writing of this book.

One of the things I noticed was that I came from a place of deep rage and trauma that has affected my life for many years since I worked at that nasty store where I got robbed all the time, but the dream I had in Rome, where I was fighting with my mom, and I finally gave up and decided to apologize and forgive her, brought me back to probably the root cause of my anger that I needed to revisit and let God heal.

I feel that that dream was a supernatural nugget of knowledge that was implanted in my soul to give me the supernatural breakthrough I needed while dreaming, which allowed me to come to a deeper realization of the causes of my shadow side and is giving me the opportunity to choose better responses moving forward.

It tied the knots perfectly with the message of the Dragon.

As I wrote this, I realized that the message of the Sasquatch, the message of the Dragon, and the message of Jesus Christ sort of go hand in hand. You decide for yourselves what fits for you.

My hope is that the life lessons of my journey will reflect in other people's lives and that my personal healing experiences from the violent trauma of the past and possibly generational trauma as well that hurt other people, which is, in essence, the story of mankind and me.

As I was ready to wrap up the writing of this book, I was asking whether the Kingdom of God or the Spiritual manifestation of our divine connection is inside or outside of us. Jesus had said it is inside, and other sources too, but religion says we have to ask and pray as if it is external to us.

The answer I received was very critical. It is inside of us when we connect with Spirit, just like it's inside an appliance when it's connected to the socket.

So, the process is that we sit, connect, and meditate, and once that connection is established, the miraculous manifestation that has no limits activates inside of us, and then it can be manifested in our world.

I hope that this book will help to shift people into a better reality for themselves inwardly by encouraging them to surrender to do their own personal inner healing work and that this healing journey will instill in us the willingness to possibly learn a new pattern of behavior but also relying on divine intervention to solidify the changes we cannot produce with our own efforts.

We can only start changing the world by healing and changing ourselves inwardly first. It's not an easy journey, but it's worth everything.

This book is specifically and spiritually written for those who are ready to hear its message and embark on their own journey of the beautiful evolution of their human soul.

CHAPTER TWENTY-SIX
So, What Does All This Lead To?

After settling back at home after my trip, I was led to write this book, and honestly, I had no idea where it would start and where it would end. I did it out of obedience, not having any experience at all.

It took me reading the book multiple times while editing (and I'm sure there are still numerous errors) to make some realizations, as the information came to me all too quickly, and the memories were overwhelming. I typed the whole book on my phone using notes. Talk about a sore thumb.

When I was almost finished writing, I decided to ask my landlady if I could have a separate internet account so I could start working remotely. I felt this was the type of work that would allow me to travel, and I did not want to start a local job and be restricted geographically.

When my landlady responded, she was about to contact me as well, and she communicated to me that she needed me to move out. This was very shocking to me as I had indicated to her that I intended to live at this property long term.

She and her husband traveled to Mexico during the winter, and this year, coming back, they were not able to find a place to rent, and they had the main house rented out. I felt that Spirit led me to ask if I had done something to offend her, and I explained my situation to her, and we came to an agreement where she offered for me to stay at a different unit.

I had just signed up for online training for remote sales work placement. I was in the middle of writing this book, and now I had to deal with possibly having to move? This did not make any sense as Spirit had told me clearly that "I would be established." Either I heard wrong, or maybe I was going to be established differently, or God was going to establish me where I was, and my spirit felt it was the latter.

At the same time, I was expecting to get paid for 5 roofing jobs that I had sold the prior year and for some money I lent to my boss, only to find out that my boss did not get paid for the whole time I was gone to Europe and had taken things to court to try to collect his wages to be able to pay me.

During that time, my ex-wife, whom I had divorced 3 times, reached out and, shortly after, started showing unhealed patterns while telling me that Bigfoot didn't exist, how the current political administration was causing all this havoc in the USA and how I needed to do all these things to protect myself which brought a lot of stress to my overall situation. I had to come to terms with knowing that "I'm a protected child of the Universe," and many will fall at my right and at my left, but I will not be harmed. It seemed as if every area of my life was under attack.

Meanwhile, I also kept receiving many uplifting and encouraging messages related to testing and blessings from the Spirit through many different sources, so I decided I would concentrate on my well-being, on my goals, on my spiritual connection and on fixing my camper van to get it ready for summer camping, only to blow the transmission just the day after I had finished restoring it. Luckily, I happen to own 3 vehicles.

This was a real-time test.

One day, as I walked out of the house, I had a conversation about my situation with the girl who rented out the main house from the owner, as where I live is a multi-unit semi-rural property. I mentioned to my neighbor that I was going to have to move to a different unit and that the owners were going to move into my unit with their dogs.

My neighbor shared with me that she had recently changed jobs and that she had bought a brand-new vehicle. During a very cold and foggy day, she slid down the road and crashed, and her new vehicle was destroyed.

She also mentioned that she felt very uncomfortable with the owners and their hired groundskeeper while I was traveling.

As we were talking, she decided she would try to prepare a purchase offer to buy the whole property.

I was able to let my neighbor borrow one of my cars and offered to sell it to her as well, but she would need to have her mechanic check it since it had belonged to my ex-wife. It's interesting how I was able to help my neighbor, and it somehow felt like a divine setup.

Over a month went by, and my neighbor drove and drove my car and did not have time to get back to me to purchase it. Spirit just told me to let her use it even though I needed the money as well.

A year prior, the Creator had put in my heart to pray about owning the portion of the property that I was renting, and I heard clearly as the Spirit told me, "Start acting like a son and ask for what you need."

That same summer, after moving into my current home, the shady groundskeeper that the owner hired did some things that made me extremely uncomfortable as well, and during that time, God told me that "I would be established where I lived."

Shortly after, I started seeing him less and less.

Since I was new to the area, I spent time checking out different communities and churches, and one Sunday, I ran into a lady at a universalist fellowship that I visited for the first time, and we had a conversation about where I moved from and where I lived. When I told her where I lived, she looked at me in disbelief and said, "You live with such and such??"

Well, as it turned out, she knew my landlady by name, and apparently, this woman had rented from my landlady and told me of a very bad situation she had been in while living at this property where she ended up being evicted and ended up homeless with her child for a year after that. She sternly warned me not to engage with the landlady too much.

Now, what are the chances that I run into the very person who could give me this information as I had just moved into town and during my first visit to a random church?

The year prior, I had been led to sell my house, move to this new state, found this rental by miracle and then, I was led to go on my trip to Europe for 3 months, and as I came back, all hell was breaking loose.

I decided I wanted to really press in with my relationship with God, and the only place that I felt led to attend was a nondenominational Christian church downtown.

No other place felt right for me, and it was big enough that I could come in, get lost in the crowd and not be seen and leave at will. I needed time to reflect on my situation and connect and hear from Spirit.

To say the least, I had come back to a hellish situation as I was also witnessing historical geopolitical events that matched the many ends of the world prophecies from so many different texts.

During this time, my dear friend from Iran, who I met in Sevilla, kept contacting me. We missed each other so much. She told me that she had finally left Spain, and she told me that Spirit led her to move to Iran. She has no religion, by the way.

While I was in Sevilla, Spirit had told me to help her financially, and she was herself in a hellish situation, living in a Spanish homeless shelter in Sevilla after her husband had passed away.

I was actually worried that her idea of moving to Iran was not too safe as the war was about to break out, but she was confident in having heard correctly from Spirit before she made such a move.

As I had mentioned earlier, my Iranian friend is a spiritual person and a psychotherapist who had been working for many years on a revolutionary inner healing method, and she was extremely grateful that I was led to help her financially, so she offered therapy for me as I was navigating all these difficult situations.

It seemed that everything, as chaotic as it was, seemed to have been pre-arranged.

After my last conversation with my ex-wife and while I was going through all these challenging situations, my Iranian friend mentioned something that really caught my attention.

She mentioned to me that she had been in an extremely abusive relationship with a man and that her breakthrough point came about when she began looking at her partner with unconditional love even in the middle of the abuse and that this action was the beginning of shadow work or inner healing work.

This coincidentally had many parallels with the teachings of Jesus Christ and the recurring messages that I received from the dragons throughout my life. I was able to see this from her perspective through my friend's therapeutic and practical perspective.

My realizations have been many folds in the sense that all the teachings I had received during my early Christian years, my experiences with other people's perspectives, and my own experiences outside of the Christian box matched those teachings in almost a seamless manner.

During the Easter service at the church where I was attending, a scripture they mentioned stood out. It was John 15:19: "The son can do nothing of his own, but he does what he sees the father do."

Now, I see the holy scriptures through a lens that goes right along with the law of attraction and manifestation but with a pearl of revelation, and I hope I can articulate it correctly.

Everything that Jesus Christ did was linked to manifestation; having faith has to do with manifestation; there were examples where people got healed, and Jesus told them, "Your faith has healed you."

You never hear him say, "I healed you," and this all proves that we indeed have a lot to do with creating our own reality.

Now, I also believe that our perception can create many alternative timelines, and as I was pondering upon my current challenges, I was forced to make a choice to either believe in God's promises and align with them or to look at my situations in hopelessness.

Well, the choice is clear, I received specific downloads of information, such as "I will be established," and I have to align that with my mind, feelings, intention and heart. And it takes a lot of focus sometimes and a lot of letting go.

So, manifestation works in two ways:

We hear the direction from the Source of all divine wisdom, and then we know what we should follow, such as my friend moving to Iran.

We act on those nuggets of direction, such as aligning with the downloads we get and things manifest for us, but we first need to connect with the Divine source. That is what Jesus taught all along. The promises of God are true, but they become activated by our alignment and our agreement, which equals faith. So, we truly are co-creators with the divine.

Now, during my trip, I was led to say prayers and open portals at many different places, and one that stood out was Rome. I followed the instructions I was given by Spirit and released prayers in light language at the Vatican, and lo and behold, just a few days ago, the Pope passed away.

Now, since my prayers were in light language, they bypass reason, so I have no idea what I prayed, but it's interesting to see that there have been some seriously insane events after those prayers since I came back home. Not only did the Pope pass away, but I heard that Claus Schwab apparently stepped down. I haven't confirmed that yet at the time of writing this.

Another thing I noticed was that there is a correlation between the dates when Pope John Paul II passed away and the release of Star Wars Episode III, "Revenge of the Sith," and the recent death of Pope Francis just days away from the release of Star Wars "Anniversary."

You can't make this up!

Both popes died on the release of 2 different episodes, which depict the stages of the struggle between the Jedi and the evil empire. Coincidence?

The way I see it is, basically, it's predictive programming. The powers that shouldn't be are using it through the media, and this shows that we are in a simulation of sorts that has been pre-planned and is being executed accordingly.

However, we are the co-creators in this reality with either the Divine or with the rulers of this world, and we must focus on aligning our intention with the personal instructions we get directly from the Source so we can manifest that reality instead.

If we are of the Light, of course. And the choice is ours.

We are the Jedi in real life. We are the resistance and the creators of the timelines we experience.

The powers that are trying to dominate us depend on our agreement. The Spirit of the Creator, who has nothing but good things for us, also depends on our agreement. That's how powerful we are, and knowing this, we need to be extremely intentional and aware of our thoughts, and we need to start taking responsibility for how we think because as we think (so are we), in other words, we manifest our reality.

Even through the struggles that we face, we must apply faith as our agreement so that we align with the best reality possible, but we cannot do it alone. That is why Jesus went directly to the Source Creator to get perspective, and he only did as he said, "As he saw the Father do."

Now, as I write this, I'm being reminded of what God told me when I got kicked out of all the churches and ended up in the metaphysical communities. I mentioned it in a previous chapter. When I asked who all these people were at the metaphysical communities, Spirit told me almost audibly, "These are my children; I want them to use my power."

What I feel that God is pointing out is that the big difference between just going through the motions of manifesting and inner healing and healing others on our own and connecting with true power is simply accessing what God referred to as "His Power" as he clearly told me he wanted His Children to run with his power, and that is what the so-called "elites" fear the most and is called "The Anointing of God," and that is the big difference.

Also, I'm being reminded of how many times I had a question for the Sasquatch only to hear them say, "Follow your inner voice," which to me points back to hearing the Divine Source as we connect and hear within ourselves.

That is what they are trying to keep us away from by causing divisions between religions, making up dogmas and distractions to keep us from focusing on the Divine itself and poisoning our food and many other things. We must access the anointing of God.

If we pay attention to the recent events with the solar flares and the Schumann resonance, this is the amplification of positive energies that are hitting humanity as a whole, and this is the fulfillment of the scriptures, which says, "I will pour out my Spirit on All Flesh" which mentions nothing about religion.

My encouragement for this challenging upcoming world season that we are entering is to make it a priority to connect with the Holy Spirit of the Creator.

Jesus gave us the blueprint, and no, he was not a religion. He was and is the Son of God, and the message I received was "These are My children," meaning we all are Sons and Daughters of God the Divine.

Our mission is to align with our own personal instructions that we receive from the Divine and to ignore the media, which has been weaponized to make us focus on creating the reality that tries to enslave us.

The very next day, after I finished writing this last chapter, I received a call from my publisher asking for payment on the remaining fees for my book. I mentioned to him that I was waiting for a check as well and I would make payment as soon as I received it.

Literally two minutes after we hung up, an online video from a random channel said the following:

"Hey guys, Papa (Meaning God Creator) said: It is a waiting game! If you can wait, you will outlast your circumstances, if you can outlast your circumstances, they will come in last. It is just a waiting game."

This is how we are taken care of and grow into our next blessing so we can handle it when it finally manifests. We are taken care of at every level, even through the discomfort of waiting.

The next day, I decided to go camping. I had moved to the state that I was shown, and the outdoor possibilities are endless here, since I had finished my book and my sales training, it was time to take a break.

Again, I was presented with a choice of focus and manifestation. As I was driving down the road, I felt the presence of the Forest People (Sasquatch) ahead of me while I was driving. When I looked to my left, I saw some huge structures, and I decided to go explore.

I took a trail up an unmarked road and came across a huge cluster of structures. It seemed that someone had been camping there as someone had left a lot of thrashes.

I normally try to clean up the forest as much as I can, but this time, there was too much to put in my car, so I just started piling up what I found.

After a few moments, I noticed several items on the ground as well as empty cans of alcoholic beverages and many other items, there were signs of some sort of target shooting on metal objects and the energy there was quite heavy. I felt this was not a safe spot. It was about to get dark, so I got on the road and found a safe spot a few miles up the road.

I spent some time clearing the energy I felt.

Again, what are the chances that the first place I feel called to explore had this right next to the Sasquatch structures?

I spent the rest of the night meditating, clearing the energy of what I had just seen, playing my instruments and eating.

I had to make a strong choice to either focus on the negative or on what spirit was showing me to do.

The next morning, I continued my journey, and as I was driving, I needed to go to the bathroom. I saw out of the corner of my eye a dirt trail and decided to turn around and go there.

After relieving myself, I kept driving down the trail and came up onto a hidden gem of a spot where I found a beautiful campsite right next to the river overlooking the snowy mountains. The previous campers were leaving as I arrived, and the timing was flawless.

I decided I was not in a hurry to get anywhere and decided to set up my camp and take advantage of this hidden spot. I still needed to process the events of the previous night.

As I was making my breakfast, a thought came to me from Spirit about the Christian meaning of "salvation." I need to share this as well, and I hope I can also share this as it's been shown to me.

I was reading some passage and then lost it when I put my phone down, but basically, the revelation I got was that "salvation" is equal to establishing a connection with the highest and purest form of the Divine source or, in other words, coming from a place of spiritual disconnection into a thriving connection with Creator."

Without this connection, we remain spiritually dead, with no divine assistance to receive the breath of eternal life and the direction we need to navigate this three-dimensional reality.

There is no religion necessary to accomplish this, but for some people, it may be necessary to have some spiritual guidance from those who have more experience, and we are all led where we can benefit the most.

However, I have to say that there is something we cannot do on our own and replicate.

I have not seen such power equal to the power of the Creator.

The whole point is that salvation equals nurturing our spiritual connection. It allows us to access the Divine breath of life and allows us to disconnect from spiritual death, which is disconnection from the Source, and this disconnection leads us to spiritual and moral decay to the point where scenes like the one I found earlier in the forest become the norm.

Just when I thought I was done writing this book, a nudge led me to meditate about Christ and how that fits into the picture.

I believe I mentioned already that during an exchange with my Native American friend, she mentioned that she specifically asked the Sasquatch if they knew about Christ.

To my amazement, what they told her was: "Yes, the one who walked on water."

She mentioned to me that they have absolute reverence towards Christ, and they call him "The One." I'm not an advocate for religion in any sense, but what came to me was that Christ truly did something similar to blood magic. Not using someone else or some animal but himself.

The whole concept of sin and shame does not sit well with me, but the concept of karmic repercussions does!

When we do things that cause us to lower our vibration, it comes down to disrespect. Disrespect of ourselves, of creation and of others. Negative actions change our DNA and can be transferred to the following generations, thus causing us unnecessary hardship. Think of the nasty scene in the forest that I found and the bad energy it released.

What Christ did was cleanse or karmic load through a blood ritual that will never be repeated nor equaled by anyone else. When we come in agreement with this event, we literally align in the quantum field with reversing that karma and bad energy in our lives, and we align with Christ's purpose of cleansing our ancestral line so we can connect with the

Source Creator without hindrance.

It is from this place of connection that we can experience power, love, inner healing, freedom, a sound mind and the ability to activate our spiritual gifts and raise the vibration necessary to heal ourselves and save humanity from self-destruction, but it starts within our own personal connection with the Divine, our own journey of healing and our own personal growth.

That afternoon camping while sitting by the river, I felt it was the day to just let go of all the weight of all the recent events and contemplate what Spirit has been doing in my life.

I'm not one to demonize how people connect with the Spirit and not one to dictate how things should be done, as I feel the Spirit will talk to us in any way we are ready to hear.

We put a box around ourselves when we limit how God will talk to us. I guess the rule of thumb is, first, we need to know the voice of the Divine. What I mean by this is that the Divine will always comfort us, guide us into all truth, build us and encourage us.

Any voice that speaks to us in any less than the highest good for our souls is more than likely not the voice of the Most High.

Some people pay attention to animals, such as the Native Americans do. Some people pay attention to numbers, some to scriptures, some to codices, but I've noticed repeatedly how the same exact message can come to me repeatedly from seemingly unrelated sources. I personally pay attention to everything.

Our job is to pay attention to the message, not judge the messengers but discern them.

I set my heart to pull some cards as I sat by the river. I shuffled my deck of angel cards from Sonia Choquette's "Ask Your Guides Oracle Cards," which I had forgotten I had stashed in my lunch box, and I felt that I needed to pull just one.

The card that I pulled was number "11 New Beginnings -Divine Father," which is on PAGE 22, and the next chapter is 12 (triple 1 and triple 2). I'm not making this up. This is crazy! See the pictures!!

Again, what are the chances that this would even happen?

New beginnings were the message of Chico De Gallo, the evolved dragon (Into a rooster) that brought me so much joy, encouragement, and love.

I guess something I have in my heart to share is that I'm not here to brag about all the amazing things that I get to experience as if I were some super-duper spiritual guru of sorts.

I'm here to encourage my readers to tune into what is already available and possible for themselves through their own Divine connection.

The following morning, after I wrote this, Spirit told me that there is an anointing for people who read this book so they can get activated spiritually. I don't know how that will happen in the lives of my readers, but I know that if you come to an agreement and ask to be upgraded spiritually with the anointing of this book, you will receive it. You just have to ask and mean it.

So, I declare that the anointing of the Most High touches you and changes your life from where you are to where you transform into the best activated, healed, humble, grateful and powerful version of yourself!

I don't have all the answers, and I'm far from knowing what the hell I'm doing half the time, like anyone else on this planet.

Just be aware that even though we are far from perfect, we have access to divine perfection in those lucid moments of spontaneous brilliance when we choose to listen to our personal inspirational guidance and take the necessary risks.

What has worked for me the most, to be able to connect with the Divine as I sit down to meditate and pray, can be summarized in one word:

Gratitude!

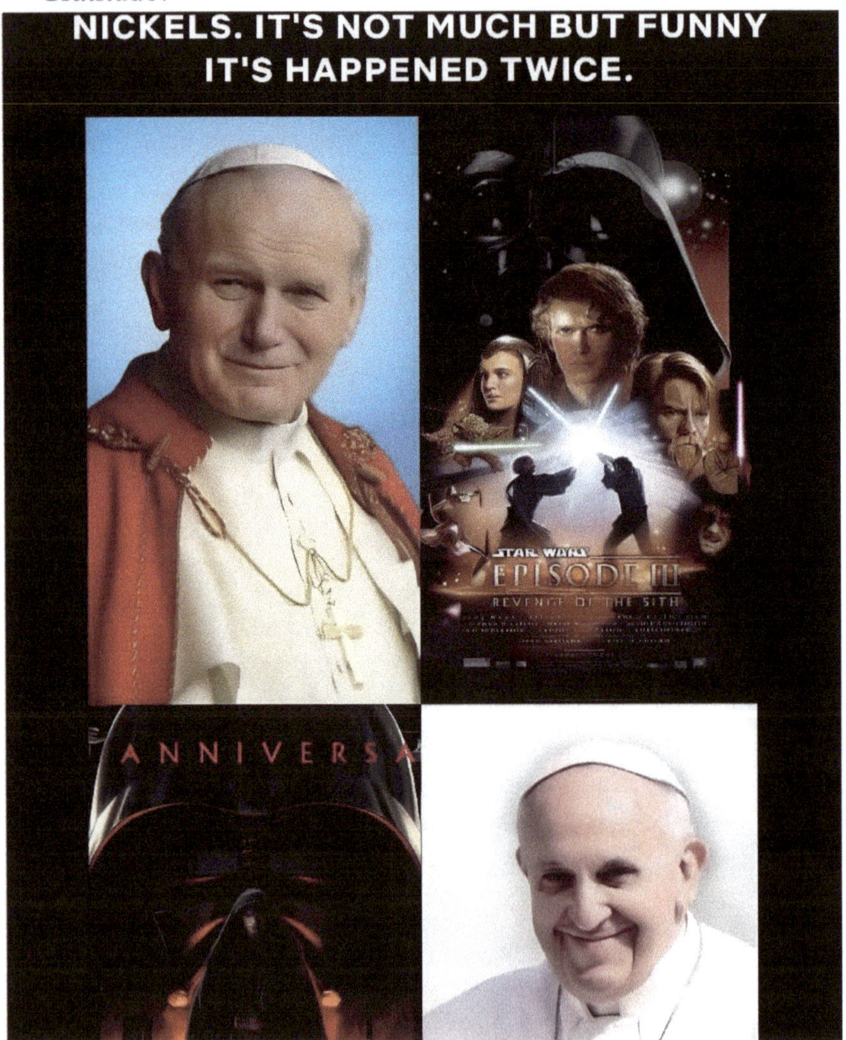